Snoggle

J. B. Priestley

Snoggle

Illustrated by Barbara Flynn

Harcourt Brace Jovanovich, Inc.

New York

Contents

Snoggle

Chapter 1

Spaceship?

It was one of those days when it looks at first as if nothing interesting can happen, but then later, when you don't expect anything, almost everything happens. August is a good time for these peculiar days, and this one was in the middle of August. The Hoopers—James, nearly sixteen, and Peg, fourteen, and Robin, thirteen—were not at school of course, but for once they were having to stay at home. It was their parents who were away, having taken the car to France and Italy.

Grandpa was here—to "look after them," as the parents said, though Peg always felt it was they who were looking after him, though she also felt she did more of it than the two boys. Not that she minded, because she loved Grandpa, who was Professor (retired) Richard Hooper, who had taught history and now wrote books about it. He was writing one now, very long and very dull, about William Pitt and the Duke of Newcastle, whoever they were. He was very old, over seventy, and had lovely white hair and eyebrows, but because he smoked a pipe all the time, he had rather too strong a smell of tobacco. Even so, though ancient, he always seemed to Peg closer to them than Daddy was. He wasn't so busy and worried and he never talked about money. Then again, though he was writing his book in the room above theirs, at the back of the house, he never complained if they made a noise.

Their playroom, which was quite big and entirely theirs, was on the ground floor, close to the kitchen and the back door of the house. All the furniture was badly worn and battered, but that was just right because they hadn't to bother about it. The chief piece—and the most useful—was an enormous cupboard, jam-packed with all their old stuff—old toys, books they no longer read, tennis rackets with half the strings gone, all kinds of junk and muck. Another good thing about this room of theirs was that you hadn't even to pop across to the back door if you wanted to slip out, because on the other side it had those huge windows that open like doors, taking you straight onto the lawn—a super arrangement.

On this particular afternoon, not very long after they had eaten their cold meat and salad and summer pudding, these window-doors were wide open, but all three of them were still indoors. The storm wasn't as bad as it had been—and there had been a lot of thunder and lightning—but it was still rolling and grumbling around. So there was no point in going out until it had really stopped. James, who was keen on tennis, was standing not far from the window, practicing his service, just swinging his racket and not using any balls. And being ridiculously solemn about it, too. Robin was lolling as best he could on the lumpy wreck of a sofa, reading a book about astronomy or space travel or something of that sort. He was so crazy about that stuff he was hardly on the earth at all except during mealtimes. Peg herself was sitting at a small table facing the window and was try-

ing to write a poem, something she often did when she couldn't go out.

She wasn't getting on very well. The thunder decided to start all over again, producing a sudden loud clap, so that she looked up and spoke to it sharply. "Oh—*do* shut up!"

"Nobody's saying anything," said James, between serves.

"I mean that silly thunder. I want to *concentrate*."

James went through a serve again. "Another poem?" he asked in a teasing tone. Then, when Peg ignored him: "About wanting to be a tree again?"

"Now—*you* can shut up," Peg told him, not angrily though. She wanted to put an end to this talk because in fact this poem *was* about a tree, though not wanting to be it. Concentration was difficult because the thunder went rolling round, even if it wasn't very loud now, and there seemed to be several distant flashes of lightning.

Robin was the next interrupter. Something he had just read had delighted him. "If you took a pinch of stuff from a White Dwarf, it might weigh tons and tons. Oh, boy!"

James was only half listening but of course felt he had to say something. "How could pinching a dwarf weigh anything?"

"Don't be *thick*," Robin told him. "I didn't say that. I said—are you listening?—"

"No."

"Neither am I," said Peg, though this wasn't quite true. But she did wish they'd shut up.

But once Robin was among the stars, he couldn't be silenced. "A White Dwarf," he began very deliberately, "is a small, old, and very, very heavy star. And just a pinch of it—a spoonful—could weigh tons and tons." This made him laugh, just because he adored it all. "One little bit of your fingernail would knock you flat." He laughed again. "Its atoms haven't any space in them—they're all sort of mashed up together. Jolly good!"

This was too much for Peg. "What's jolly good about it?"

"Hear, hear!" cried James, right in the middle of a serve.

Robin was disgusted with them. "OK—OK—OK— you're not interested. Well, I *am*." He began reading again.

And now because he wanted to be quiet, James and Peg had to start teasing him. "A hundred million stars in our galaxy," said James in a singsong tone.

Peg couldn't resist joining in, using the same tone. "And millions and millions of galaxies." And then, sounding deeply disgusted: "*Ugh!*"

This pulled in Robin. "*Ugh* yourself! It's a very big universe, that's all."

"It's too big," said Peg. "It's disgusting and frightening."

"You only say that because it makes you feel like nothing—"

This annoyed Peg. "And you're only on its side because you like astronomy and space travel and all that. Anyhow, I'm *not* nothing. I'm Peg Hooper, Laurel Lodge, Mitchling, Wiltshire, England, Earth."

"Turn it up a minute, Peg," said James. "Watch this service, both of you. Now then—*Hooper to serve for the match*. Watch! *Slam, bang, wham!* Another ace—eh?"

Robin, who had looked up from his book to watch, was serious now. "No, James—sorry—but that one would have gone straight into the net."

"I don't think so. Do you, Peg?"

She shook her head. "Honestly I don't know—can't tell."

"Well, I can," said Robin, who probably could, too. "And I say it wouldn't have gotten over the net because you're not reaching high enough, James. But then it's useless practicing your serve without a ball and a net."

"It's a lot of use—to get the right rhythm. But of course," James continued solemnly, "as soon as it's fine and the court's dried off, then I'll do my serve there. But I'll try reaching a bit higher. Watch!"

This is when it really all began. There was first a strange whirring sound. Then there was a flicker of odd light in the sky, which Peg and Robin might not have noticed if they hadn't been looking toward James and the window.

"UFO!" cried Robin, bounding up from the sofa and then running outside.

"Oh, rats!" James looked and sounded disgusted. "What's the matter with *him?*"

Peg's reply came rather uncertainly. "I don't know, I don't know, James. But there was something queer out there—a noise and a light—"

"It was just the end of the storm, that's all." And James didn't even bother to turn round and see where Robin was.

Peg didn't want to get into the middle of a quarrel between her brothers. Even so, she couldn't entirely give in to James. "I don't think it *was* the end of the storm. The noise was different. So was the light."

"Bilge!" James was still disgusted, perhaps because he wouldn't go out to look and yet couldn't go on with his serving.

"Robin's coming back, all het up."

"More bilge now—"

"I think it was a UFO," Robin announced, rather squeakily because he was excited.

"A what?" Peg really didn't know what he was talking about.

"UFO. An Unidentified Flying Object." Robin was very grand about this.

"You mean," said James, even deeper in disgust now, "one of those flying saucers people think they see? That's out. Don't be batty."

"I'm not being batty—*you* are," Robin replied hotly. Then he was off. "Because a lot of people have seen things that weren't there—or weather balloons—or experimental planes they didn't see properly, that doesn't mean there couldn't be a flying saucer—a spaceship." As the other two tried to interrupt: "Oh—*do* shut up—and listen. I know a lot more about it than you two—"

He might have gone on about this, but he didn't because at that moment Grandpa joined them. Looking at them above his spectacles, which were always sliding down his nose, Grandpa said mildly, "Well now, what's happening here?"

Being the eldest, James replied. "I'm sorry if we disturbed you, Grandpa."

"It was my fault," said Robin, who apart from galaxies and spaceships and all that stuff was a fair-minded, good-hearted boy.

"It was all of us," Peg declared, even though she didn't believe she was to blame.

But there wasn't to be any blaming. "No, no, you didn't disturb me. I've come down to ask a question. You see, instead of working on the elder William Pitt and the

Duke of Newcastle, I was staring out of the window—a bad habit of mine. And then I heard a rather strange sound and saw a curious flash of light—"

"There you are, James!" Robin almost shrieked.

"Wasn't it just the end of the storm, Grandpa?"

"No, I don't think it was, you know, James. Something quite different." And Grandpa took out his pipe, looked at it as if it might turn into something else, and then said slowly, "Quite different."

"Yes it was." This was Peg, who didn't like to be left out.

"All right then, Grandpa," said James, "but now Robin's off about flying saucers and spaceships—"

"And the next thing," cried Peg, "it'll be millions and millions of stars again—billions and billions of miles of empty space—and all that. And Robin knows I *hate* it."

Grandpa gave her one of his slow grins. "I'm not very fond of it myself. Cheerless, I always feel. But Robin, perhaps because he's the youngest of us, seems to belong to the space age. Your turn then, Robin."

"OK—and thanks, Grandpa! Now didn't you agree the other night that spaceships might have landed here, before there were so many people, and then taken off again?" And Robin gave him an appealing look. "You did, didn't you?"

Being so old and having been a professor for so long, Grandpa answered this kind of question very cautiously. "Well, I did say it wasn't impossible, even though most of the evidence would be against it. The immense distances —and so forth. And there's something else I pointed out. If creatures on some other planet were clever enough to be able to pay us a visit, they'd probably be clever enough to know we aren't worth visiting."

Peg gave him a reproachful look. "Oh—Grandpa—aren't we?"

"Speaking as an old historian, my dear, I doubt if we are. If these clever advanced creatures put it to me, I'm afraid I'd have to advise them to stay away."

"There you are, Robin," said James.

But Robin refused to be *there,* wherever it was. "But they might land here by accident—or to refuel or something—or send back a report on the earth's surface.

Just the way we do—with Mars and Venus—only much better, landing a big spaceship, coming from another part of the galaxy—"

"Robin, *please*," cried Peg, "don't start that all over again. Grandpa, tell him not to. I mean, things with eight eyes and a lot of what's-it—tentacles. Sooner or later I'll begin dreaming about them."

Grandpa was relighting his pipe, something he was always doing, but he managed to make some sort of noise that stopped the boys from breaking in. "No, we won't have any monsters, Peg. And I don't propose to accept your spaceship, Robin. But at the same time—and this is why I came down—I can't help feeling that something very odd, very unusual indeed, happened—and not very far away. Being upstairs, I must have been more aware of it than you were."

Robin was all eagerness. "Yes of course, Grandpa. So what did you see?"

This made Grandpa careful again. He made use of his pipe very cleverly. "Nothing clearly." Puff, puff, puff. "There was this flashing light—a bluey-green, I'd say." Puff, puff. "And I did get the impression that something I couldn't see properly at all came down"—puff, puff—"and then perhaps hovered a little before it vanished."

"Spaceship." And Robin announced this as if the thing were waiting to come into the room.

"But then I may have been deceiving myself," Grandpa told him. "We're always deceiving ourselves. History is largely a record of self-deception."

Peg, who was nearest, heard a banging on the back door and slipped out to open it. "Oh—hello!" she said, with no enthusiasm.

"Hello!" said Mrs. Bing-Birchall, who came in without being asked and then pushed past Peg. She was a large, bony, shouting kind of woman, whom the boys disliked just as much as Peg did.

"Oh—good afternoon! I'm Mrs. Bing-Birchall—"

"This is our grandfather—Professor Hooper," Peg announced.

Grandpa was now standing up. "How d'you do, Mrs. Birchall?"

"No, it's *Bing*-Birchall," the woman shouted. "There's a hyphen."

"I'm so sorry," said Grandpa. "I've always had trouble with hyphens. Is there anything—"

"I had to come round to this door because I couldn't make anybody hear at the front door," Mrs. Bing-Birchall complained, louder than ever.

If she expected Grandpa to be genuinely sorry about this, she was unlucky. He replied quite cheerfully. "The bell's out of order, I'm afraid—and we were all in here. My son and daughter-in-law are abroad, and they left me in charge here—if you can call it that—"

"But isn't there something wrong with your phone, too? Because I tried that first. No go." And she gave Grandpa a very severe look.

Cheerful as before, Grandpa said, "Yes, I believe something has gone wrong with the telephone. No telephone—no front doorbell—not good organization—"

"Well," Mrs. Bing-Birchall replied, "I wasn't going to say it, but now that you've said it, I couldn't agree with you more."

"These three are too young to care about good organization, and I'm too old. Middle life is the organizing time.

That's why it's so worrying. But you're a neighbor, I imagine, Mrs. Bing-Birchall," Grandpa continued, "so is there anything we can do for you?"

"Had an urgent sort of call on the phone from Major Rodpath," she replied. "And as my old bus is in dock, I've come running round to see if I could cadge a lift or borrow your car. Don't tell me the Hoopers have taken it abroad."

"I'm afraid they have, you know. Would a bicycle do —rather small and battered, I fear—"

"No, thanks. I'll pop back and phone Alan Rodpath. If it's all that important, he can run round in his car and pick me up." She shouted at everybody now and not just at Grandpa. "Poor old Roddy seems to be in a flap about something but didn't say what."

When there was a visitor the boys disliked, they had a trick, which Peg could never quite manage, of shutting themselves in themselves so that they were not only silent but almost invisible. But now Robin came out of it—calm and clear. Looking Mrs. Bing-Birchall in the eye, he said, "It's a spaceship."

"Not funny, dear!" she told him.

"I'm not trying to be funny. Am I, Grandpa?"

"No, you're not. He's not, Mrs. Bing-Birchall."

James emerged now. "But I'll believe it's a spaceship when I see it—"

"Quite right, Jimmy—it *is* Jimmy, isn't it?"

He was very firm with her. "No, Mrs. Bing-Birchall. It's *James*."

"Same thing, surely?"

Grandpa wagged his head at her. "No, not if he feels like James and not like Jimmy."

Peg felt it was her turn. "I've always felt like Peg and not Margaret—"

"Have you, dear?" the woman shouted at her. It's not easy to show no interest at all and yet still shout, but Mrs. Bing-Birchall could do it. "Well, all very fascinating —but I must buzz off and phone Major Rodpath. After all, he couldn't be in such a flap about *nothing*." She offered Robin a madly condescending smile. "Even if we can't offer you a spaceship, young man. Bye-bye, everybody! As the telephone girls used to say—*Sorry you've been troubled.*"

She was off before Peg could do anything about doors. It was very quiet after she'd gone. Nobody said anything for a minute or two. They all just enjoyed her not being there. Then Grandpa looked at his watch.

"As you know," he began, "I don't usually work in the afternoon, but I had to spend this morning reading, and I want to rough out this chapter while the stuff's still in my head. Does the woman from the village—Mrs. What's-her-name—come this afternoon?"

"No, she's finished today. And it's my turn to make tea. Will you be coming down for it, Grandpa?"

"At the moment, I think not, but in an hour's time I may think differently. And don't bother telling me you don't like Mrs. Bing-Bang. I realized at once you didn't." He nodded, grinned, then left them.

James went to look outside. "It's clearing up. I'll give it a few more minutes, then I'll go down to the court and try my serves there. Anybody interested?"

"Spaceship for me," Robin declared. "Not tennis balls."

"Well, you're quite right just to sit here and find it,"

said James. "Because all you're doing is imagining it."

"How do *you* know, you chump? You heard what Grandpa said? He saw *something* come down."

"And what's he doing about it? Nothing," James announced triumphantly. "He's just gone up to think about William Pitt and the Duke of Newcastle again. That shows he didn't *really* believe anything important had happened."

"I remember thinking that," Peg told them.

"But why did Major Thing—Rodpath—phone Mrs. Bing-Birchall?"

"Oh—come off it, Robin!" cried James. "He's in a flap because he's heard a chap's been seen shooting a pheasant—or some rot these shooting types are keen on."

"If I was going to shoot anything," said Peg rather dreamily, "I think I'd shoot Mrs. Bing-Birchall—not to kill her but put her in the hospital for months. I simply can't *bear* her. The way she pushed past me, just walking in! And now she's ruined my poem. I'm in the wrong mood. All her fault."

"Well then, don't bother about being a tree again," James told her. "Write a *hate* poem. Call it *To Mrs. Bing-Bang.*" And both boys, unlike Peg, thought this very funny.

When they had finished their silly chortling, Peg said with dignity, "I don't write hate poems. Poetry shouldn't be about hating."

"What about that one on the gym mistress?" said Robin.

"I was younger then."

James had found some tennis balls. "Well, I'm going down to the court. What my serve needs now is not only speed but spin. Anybody interested will be welcome." He went out through the open French windows. Peg began to read over what she had already written, and Robin, on the sofa, returned to his book. But of course Robin couldn't keep quiet for long.

"If you set out for the nearest galaxy—not ours of course but the next one, the very nearest—it would take you—"

Peg cut him short. "Don't tell me. I don't want to know. I haven't to bother about galaxies."

"I call that a very stupid attitude." Robin was very lofty.

"What about you?"

"*What* about me?" Robin demanded, his face rather red as it always was when he was getting cross.

"You pretend to believe a spaceship's landed. But all the same, you just sit there—reading. Why aren't you rushing out, looking for it? Shall I tell you?"

"No." And he pretended he'd stopped listening.

Peg could be very persistent sometimes. "Because you're afraid you won't find one—and then you'll feel disappointed."

Robin looked at her. "Rather clever—but not true."

"Robin Hooper—are you *sure?*"

He nodded, very solemn now. "Now just you listen carefully, Peg. And this is *confidential*. What you're forgetting is that I did rush out, just as the thing was landing. And I ran straight up to the top of our little hill—to get a better view. Now it's true it might have landed miles and miles away—"

"I thought of that, too," Peg said hastily.

"But I don't think it did. And don't forget Major Rodpath's flapping about *something*. Now this is what I believe, though I didn't want to say anything to James because he'd only laugh. I believe the spaceship landed —and not very far from here—and that as soon as it landed it became invisible—or just a faint blur. And not only that. If you tried to get close to it, you couldn't. It would use some kind of force to keep you away."

All this seemed a bit much to Peg. "How d'you know?"

"Well, I don't for certain, you silly sausage. But if I was clever enough to bring a spaceship billions and billions of miles, I know that's what I'd do first, make it invisible and then protect it with some kind of force, some sort of electric barrier—until I knew that people here were friendly. See?"

"Up to a point, Robin. But it means you have to believe an awful lot, doesn't it?"

"OK, OK! But it does explain why I'm still sitting here and not rushing out, trying to find something that's already invisible and not getatable. I'm sitting here," he continued rather grandly, "waiting for developments."

As he said that, he stared hard at Peg, who didn't want any developments—unless of course the spaceship just went away—and told him so. "But then," she concluded, "you could be making it all up, couldn't you, Robin?"

"No, I couldn't," he shouted, scarlet-faced. "And you'll see. I bet you anything there'll be developments."

Peg disliked being shouted at. "Where've you gotten this *developments* from? It isn't our kind of word. Like town-planning and all that stuff."

"OK, I'm not mad about it myself. But you know what I mean. Something's bound to happen soon."

And for once he was quite right.

Chapter 2

The Creature

It was only a few minutes later when they heard James, at some distance, calling Robin urgently.

"James is shouting for you, Robin," said Peg.

"I know. I heard him. It's a trick to get me down to the court. Not on."

"Well, I think if he shouts for me, I'll go." Peg was finding it impossible to get back to the poem. "It's a bit mean to keep away when he's working so hard on his service. Listen!"

"Nothing doing!"

But now James was much closer. "Robin! Robin! SOS. Mayday, Mayday!"

"This isn't tennis," cried Peg, jumping up. Robin was close behind her as they hurried out, and now James, sweating and out of breath, was only a few yards away.

"Come on, you chump!" James, who needed it, took a deep breath. "It's a creature—and you've got to give me a hand with it—not you, Peg, you'd be no use anyhow—you wouldn't want to touch it—"

So she hesitated as Robin darted forward. "What sort of creature?" she heard Robin ask.

James was already moving away and shouting over his shoulder. "You'll see. Fantastic!"

"Spaceship?" Robin was all excitement.

"Could be. Peg, you tell Grandpa."

She ran upstairs and found Grandpa already looking out of his window. "I've just heard the boys shouting," he explained. "Let's see what's happening." So they hung out of the window together and could see and hear the boys quite plainly. They were standing over a roundish something that appeared to gleam and even glitter in the sunlight.

James said, "I thought it was pegging out when I left it to call you. But it's much nearer than it was, so it can still move a bit."

Robin was taking a closer look. "Perhaps it isn't a creature at all—just some kind of little machine—"

"No, it's alive, Robin, but only just. It rolled its eyes at me when I first saw it—"

"A machine might be able to do that—"

"I tell you, it's alive. And we've got to move it into the house—either by pushing it or carrying it."

Stare as she might, Peg could hardly see anything of the creature now as both boys were bending over it.

"And now you can stop laughing at me, James," Robin was saying. "I say this creature's come out of the spaceship."

"It might have done—at that," James admitted.

"You can see it's not an earth creature at all," cried Robin, squeaky with excitement. "Look—it's opening its eyes. They're jolly big but they're eyes all right—so that's *something*. And I think it *wants* us to help it."

"I'm sure it does," said James. "I felt that as soon as I

saw it." He turned and looked up. "Hoy—Grandpa! Come down and help."

"Coming!" Grandpa shouted. He went down first and at a surprising speed, too. Peg followed him but was not in such a hurry. She was divided between curiosity and an excusable fearfulness. One moment she felt it was a rather pathetic creature that needed help, and the next moment she wondered if it wasn't some strange little monster that might do something terrible. The result was that by the time she reached the middle of their room, Grandpa was outside, helping the boys. "If it can still use those feet or paws and we take some of its weight," Grandpa was saying, "we can at least get it into the house. Now then—all together!"

As the three of them, pushing and pulling and half carrying the creature, which seemed to be terribly heavy, brought it into the room, Peg couldn't help backing away. Finally, they got it into the middle of the room and stood away from it, to take a good look at it. That was what Peg wanted to do, so she moved forward, slowly and nervously, until she was standing behind Grandpa but a little to one side of him, so that she could see properly. The creature seemed frightening at first because it was so utterly strange, but the longer she stared at it, the more *interesting* and the less frightening it appeared to her.

To begin with, there was a Humpty Dumpty look about it. That was because it had no separate head and body and was more or less egg-shaped. But it had two short, thick legs and big, flattish paws. At the other end, growing out of its egg head-body, were two pairs of fat little mast-things. Nearly halfway down its head-body were its eyes—only two of them, thank goodness!—and

these were enormous, easily the largest eyes Peg had ever
seen, three or four inches across. They didn't bulge at all
but were set quite flat in a curious way. She could hardly
see them at first because they were hidden by lids that
came down like pale green shutters. But they were rather
splendid when you did see them—dark green but somehow brilliant. The creature itself was about three feet
high, and its head-body at its widest was perhaps about
two feet across. It didn't seem to have anything like a
mouth, a nose, or ears, and this of course helped the egg
effect. Its skin—if you could call it skin—was rather like a
snake's or lizard's, only more metallic, but not at all like
hard, thick metal, if only because it kept changing color
slightly. And somehow Peg began to feel that the creature was quite unlike a machine thing that might suddenly start running around. It was feeling helpless and almost completely exhausted. So she stopped hiding behind
Grandpa and went a little nearer.

"I'm sure it's a living creature—from another planet,"
said Robin.

James looked at Grandpa. "What do you think,
Grandpa?"

"I'm inclined to believe that Robin's right," Grandpa
told him.

"Well, wherever it comes from," said James, "it's now
in a bad way—poor beast. I felt that from the first. It
seemed to give me an appealing look."

The creature's queer eyelids flickered. Peg went a little closer still. It opened its tremendous eyes, gave her a
look, then closed them again.

"Did you see?" Peg cried in high excitement. "It gave
me such a sweet, sad look. Perhaps it's hungry and we
ought to find it something to eat."

"Sorry, Peg—but that's out," Robin told her.

"Why? It *looks* hungry."

"Even if it was, we wouldn't know how to feed it."

"Doesn't seem to have a mouth," said James.

"Oh—poor thing!" cried Peg. "Well, what can we do? Grandpa, I'm sure it's miserable and *suffering*. Look at it!"

"I know, Peg," said Grandpa. "For some reason or other, the poor creature's feeling exhausted."

"I knew that from the first." This was James repeating himself. "But I can't imagine what we can do to help it."

Peg almost danced with impatience. "He might *die* soon. And I vote from now on we say *he* and not *it*. Grandpa, do think of something."

"I'm trying to, my dear." He stopped to think a moment or two. "Well now, let's suppose he really has just arrived from some distant planet, quite different from ours—"

"And he has, you know, Grandpa," Robin put in earnestly—"he really has."

"Now I seem to remember—in Wells's *War of the Worlds*—the Martians all died because our bacteria and germs and whatnot fastened onto them—and of course they hadn't our immunity—"

But Robin, the expert, wouldn't have that. "It didn't happen at once, Grandpa. It took months and months—and this creature's only just arrived. So we can wash that out."

"Right. Bacteria washed out. Well now—let's think."

They thought. Then Peg had an idea. "Perhaps the poor thing can't breathe properly."

"And I'll bet she's right, Grandpa," cried Robin. "Just

when you think Peg hasn't a clue about anything, she jumps ahead of you."

"I know, I know. So now we run and catch up with her. Let's suppose our atmosphere isn't quite right. It can't be all wrong or he'd be dead by this time."

"Also he'd have had some sort of space suit," said Robin. "Like going to the moon and taking your own oxygen. And what about oxygen? Perhaps we haven't enough for him in our atmosphere."

James pulled a face. "We can't start feeding him oxygen in this house. We'd have to take him to a hospital."

"Wait a minute, wait a minute!" Robin shouted, as if the others were about to go somewhere. "What if it's the opposite? What if we've rather more oxygen in our atmosphere than he's used to?"

"It's just possible," said Grandpa. "And at least it's something we can try out ourselves—"

"We make a stuffy atmosphere. Come on, James, Peg. And you watch him, Grandpa, while we shut everything up."

The three of them rushed about now, not only closing the French windows and the two doors, but also stuffing old newspapers into any cracks. Soon, Peg thought, it would be awfully stuffy in here. "Is anything happening?" she asked Grandpa.

"No," he replied. "Not yet. Too early anyhow."

Peg felt miserable. "Perhaps it's all wrong and we're *killing* him."

Robin came to have a look. "Give us a chance, Peg. He doesn't seem any worse."

"I think he looks a shade better," said James. "Smoke hard, Grandpa. That'll make it stuffier."

"So I've often been told, my boy." And Grandpa relit his pipe and blew out a lot of smoke.

After a few moments, Peg cried delightedly, "Look—look—look!" though in fact they *were* looking. The creature had slowly raised his body-head, apparently because he was feeling less exhausted, and he had opened his eyes to take a slow look round.

"He's feeling a bit better," James announced, almost as if he were the creature's doctor, just because he'd been the first to see him.

This wasn't good enough for Peg. "A lot better, if you ask me. And hasn't he got wonderful eyes?" Now she ventured to address the creature directly. "You're a very peculiar shape, I must admit, but your eyes are marvelous —super!" No sooner had she said that than he slowly closed his eyes again. "Oh—dear! Perhaps it's not going to work after all. Grandpa—Robin—what d'you think we ought to do now?"

"We could take him down to the coal cellar," said Robin.

"Oh no—that's a beastly idea. Even if he recovered, he'd feel so miserable."

Grandpa stopped puffing so hard. "We'll have to try something more drastic, to give him a chance to recover."

"You mean—to make it stuffier still for him?" James asked.

"Just for the time being, until he feels better. We could put him into this cupboard." But all three were shaking their heads at him. "No? Why not?"

"It's jam-packed with all our rubbish," cried James.

"Take us quarter of an hour to clear it," Robin added.

"And we can't afford to wait as long as that," said Peg. "Think of something else, Grandpa."

He took out his pipe and frowned at it—as if it ought to be giving him an idea. Then he said slowly, "We'll have to cover him with something—just for the time being."

"And I know exactly what we need," said Robin, who then made hastily for the door that led to the hall and upstairs.

Peg was a bit ungrateful for this hurry-scurry. "It's because he thinks a spaceship comes into this that Robin's so mad keen. If this poor thing had simply escaped from a zoo, he wouldn't bother at all."

"He'd be still reading," said James. "But though I haven't completely bought the spaceship idea yet, I can't see this creature coming out of a zoo."

"No, not unless somebody's running a secret weird zoo," Grandpa suggested.

James loved this idea. "A kind of horror-film zoo, full of monsters that some mad scientists have invented—"

"Stop it!" said Peg. Then she looked at the creature. "And you're not a monster really, are you? Just different."

James did his American act: "And you can say that again, Miss Hooper." He pulled a silly face at Peg, who pulled one back at him.

Robin now came charging in with a large rug from upstairs and the old telescope. "This rug ought to do nicely. Not too heavy. But I think we ought to move him back a bit first. Grandpa—James—"

The three of them half pushed, half carried the creature toward the space between the cupboard and the windows, though still keeping him well away from the wall. Peg would have helped to move him if she'd been asked, though she couldn't quite feel ready yet to touch him. But he hadn't opened his eyes again, and she felt anxious. "Don't hurt him—please!"

"He's OK," said James. "Doesn't mind a bit."

"He's a very solid, heavy sort of creature, y'know," Robin told her. "You'd soon find that out if you tried lifting him. I think he's about right there. So now for the rug."

They covered the creature with the rug, arranging it so that it was just an inch or two off the floor all round.

"He oughtn't to come to any harm there," said Grandpa. "But of course we'll have to keep taking a peep at him."

"Well, I thought you and Peg could do that, Grandpa, while James and I go out and scout round a bit. There might be one or two other creatures roaming about. That's why I brought the old telescope."

"You'll never see a thing through that telescope," Peg declared, not without scorn. "I never have."

"I'm better at it than you are," said Robin. "And it's all we have. The field glasses went off with the parents. You're coming, aren't you, James?"

"I am, but you can keep the telescope—"

"All right, my lads," said Grandpa in a sort of hearty-skipper style. "Off you go. But not too far, and don't be out too long. We have a responsibility on our hands—with poor Humpty Dumpty there. And you'd better use the back door because we don't want to redo all the cracks round those French windows. Oh—and one other thing, boys. Just keep an eye out for earth-people as well as for creatures from outer space. Mrs. Bing-Bang might be roaming round with a double-barreled shotgun."

"Affirmative," cried James.

"Roger—and out," said Robin.

The Creature

A few moments after the boys had gone, Peg, who had been thinking, announced, "But *not* Humpty Dumpty. That's not right for him."

"What? Oh—you mean for our friend under the rug. That was just a mere casual reference, my dear. I wasn't trying to christen him!"

"But he ought to have a name."

"More convenient, certainly."

"Friendlier, too," Peg continued. "And if we give him a name, then perhaps he'll answer to it."

"I wouldn't bank on that, Peg. I don't see how we'd get it through to him. Still, you think of a name."

"All right." But it wasn't all right at once. She had to work at it for nearly a minute. Then, smiling across at Grandpa, she announced the name. "Snoggle."

"Snuggle?" Grandpa was surprised.

"No, not Snuggle. He's not cuddly enough for that—"

"He's not cuddly at all, I'd say, Peg."

"It's Snoggle. *Oggle* not *Uggle*."

Grandpa nodded. "I have it now. Any particular reason for Snoggle?"

"He looks like a Snoggle."

"If there's a reply to that, I've never been able to think of it."

Peg went nearer to Snoggle under his rug, bent down, and, without lifting the rug, listened hard. "I hope he's all right, Grandpa. I can't hear him breathing."

"I've never heard him breathing." Grandpa wagged a finger at her. "You're beginning to think he's a kind of egg-shaped dog. And he isn't. He's not any kind of animal we know at all. Something quite different."

Peg returned to her chair. "Will you take a look at him soon, please, Grandpa?"

35

"Yes, but we'll give him another minute or two."

After some moments of silent wondering, Peg said, "But if Snoggle's something quite different, where does he come from and how did he get here?"

"I'm sorry, my dear, but I haven't the least glimmer of a notion."

"But you can't believe in Robin's spaceship—"

"I don't want to," he replied. "Doesn't seem likely— reasonable. But it did sound and look as if something came down. And I'm not like Robin—expecting spaceships. I'm all for keeping ourselves well away from science fiction."

"So am I. But do take a peep at Snoggle now, Grandpa."

He went across, with Peg following him. Groaning a bit, he got down on his knees and then lifted the rug in front, fairly high so that he could stare at Snoggle. He also put the hand not holding the rug inside, nearer Snoggle.

"Hoy! Steady!" He sounded really alarmed. This frightened Peg, but before she could say anything, Grandpa spoke in a quite different tone. "All right, Snoggle. I see—no harm intended. Just suggesting you feel very much better. Well, we'll have you out of that rug very soon." He dropped the rug down, got up in his ancient, groaning way, then turned and smiled at Peg.

"*Is* he feeling very much better?"

"He must be," said Grandpa. "His eyes are open—and he looks almost lively—for a Snoggle."

"But why did you cry out like that? I thought he must have bitten you."

"Come, come, my dear—you must remember he's a

Snoggle not a doggle. He's nothing to bite with. What he did was to put his paw or foot on my hand. It startled me because it felt so peculiar. Very cold, and not like skin and not like metal—something in between—"

Peg made a face. "I'd hate it if now he turned out to be just a machine—"

"I don't think he is. And his putting his paw over my hand wasn't accidental. I believe he meant it as a friendly gesture—I really do, Peg."

She jumped up in her excitement. "Instead of shaking hands—paw pressing! But that's marvelous. He was telling you he was feeling better. Why—quite soon we might be able to teach him to understand some words."

"Possibly—possibly! But you really must understand he's very different from any creature we've ever known."

"Yes, I know, I know," Peg began rather impatiently. But then she stopped—to point and then cry in triumph, "Oh—look—look!"

Somehow Snoggle had been able to move the rug from inside, and now here he was, with his eyes wide open. In her first excitement and enthusiasm, Peg told him it was wonderful and that he was a clever, clever Snoggle and must be much better. All the same she couldn't help feeling, now that she really saw him again, that he was a very strange creature indeed. While he had been hidden under the rug, she had begun to imagine, as Grandpa had suggested, that he was only an odd kind of pet, but that was no use now. She could even wonder—and this was depressing—if he wasn't really some sort of machine thing. She was just about to say something to that effect to Grandpa when Snoggle himself stopped her, for now his eyes, instead of looking at nothing, moved from her to Grandpa and then back again several times.

"You see, Grandpa!" she cried, all enthusiastic once more. "He's telling us he feels much better."

As soon as she said that, she heard the back door open, and then James and Robin came clattering back.

Chapter 3

Major Rodpath Calls

"His name's Snoggle now," Peg told the boys hastily, "and he came out of the rug himself—and he's telling us he's feeling much better."

It was just as if she hadn't spoken, as if she wasn't really there, for without a word or even a look James and Robin hurried across and began covering Snoggle with the rug again. Peg was furious.

"Don't do that, you idiots. He doesn't need it now. Stop it!"

But they grabbed hold of her as soon as she tried to take the rug away. "Shut up—and listen, Peg," said Robin very urgently.

"We've just seen that shooting type—Major Who's-it—Rodpath," said James.

"He's carrying a gun—"

"And we think he's on his way here—"

"But he wouldn't shoot Snoggle," cried Peg, horrified.

"We're not giving him a chance, are we, James?"

"No fear! And he was only about two hundred yards away, crossing the field. He'll be here in a minute," James continued, "and we haven't time now to hide what-d'you-call-him—"

"Snoggle," said Peg firmly. And if the boys didn't like it, they could lump it.

"Snoggle then. So back he goes under the rug."

"And if he starts coming out again," said Robin, "we've had it. So mind what you say, Peg."

"All right. But this is *awful*." She turned to Grandpa. "Surely he wouldn't shoot Snoggle, would he!"

"I don't know." Grandpa sounded rather sad. "But I think we'd better assume that he might. We're always shooting each other now—so why not a Snoggle? Hello—what's that?"

"Somebody at the back door," said Robin.

"Probably Major Rodpath," said James. "He would bang away like that. We'll close up to hide Snoggle, Robin. You'd better let him in, Grandpa."

"Careful then, everybody." But Grandpa wasn't being very careful himself, because on his way to the back door he didn't quite close the door of their room. And Peg felt she daren't shut it herself, not yet, though she did move nearer to it, if only to listen.

"Name's Rodpath—Major Rodpath," she heard him say. "Mind if I come in, sir? Official business—I'm a J.P. —and rather urgent."

"Is it?" said Grandpa. "What a pity! Well, let's go along to the drawing room and then you can explain."

"Certainly. After you, sir."

Peg heard them moving past the door, which meant that in a minute Snoggle would be out of danger, but then James produced one of his enormous lunatic sneezes, for which he was notorious in the family. And just to make it worse, Robin cried, "Shut up, you idiot!"

The footsteps stopped. "People in there—surely?" said Major Rodpath.

"Only my three grandchildren I'm supposed to be looking after. By the way, I'm Professor Hooper—"

"Quite, quite! Mrs. Bing-Birchall put me in the picture here. Parents away—and all that. Well—can't leave the youngsters out. Very important they should understand. So in we go!"

And in he came, with poor Grandpa, looking rather flustered now, following him. Making the best of a rotten bad job, Peg tried to give this invader a smile, but her face wasn't playing. He probably thought she had a toothache. But then Major Rodpath wasn't her kind of man at all. He had a sort of half-leathery, half-ratty face, with an untidy moustache that he seemed to want to chew when he wasn't talking. He didn't shout, like Mrs. Bing-Birchall—he barked. And he was one of those oldish men who wear thick tweed coats with bits of leather sewn on them. But what was really horrid about him was that he had field glasses round his neck, to look for anything to shoot, and was carrying a large shotgun to shoot it with. However, he did put down the gun before he talked to them.

"Carry on, shall I, Professor? Good!" He gave them a rather squinting look all round. "Got some surprising news for you chaps. Very serious. No joke at all, though I thought it was when the police first told me. I'm a magistrate. So all quite official." Two large yellow teeth moved up toward the moustache.

"Spaceship!" Robin yelled.

This was stupid of Robin because obviously Major Rodpath wanted to announce it himself. Now he looked rather put out and was probably already prejudiced against Robin. "Now who told you, boy?"

"I guessed it was." Robin was going into a squeak

with excitement. "And my grandfather thought he saw something coming down."

"I happened to be looking out of my window upstairs—"

"See it clearly?" the Major demanded.

"No, not at all. Just a vague *something* coming down."

"Pity!" It's not easy to turn *Pity!* into a bark, but Major Rodpath could do it. "Nobody's very clear," he went on. "Saucer kind of thing, they say mostly. Quite hefty—"

"Gosh!" from Robin of course.

"About three hundred feet in diameter, two fellas say. Jilks the farmer and one of his men working in a field not far away. Unreliable, both of 'em. And no check because as soon as it landed, thing became invisible."

"Gosh! That's clever." More Robin.

Major Rodpath squinted hard at him. "Clever no doubt—but sinister and dam' dangerous, if you ask me."

"But, Major," said Grandpa, "are you sure it's there?"

"Know exactly where it is. Official information. On that wasteland equidistant between Mitchling, Farfield, and Kettleton. Had two careful separate reports. Can't see it—tried myself, naturally. *And*—believe it or not—you can't get near it."

"Oh—*gosh!*"

This really annoyed Major Rodpath. "What's *your* name, boy?"

"I'm Robin, sir. Robin Hooper."

"Well, don't keep saying *Gosh* like that. Begin to think you're on their side, not ours."

"Robin happens to be very fond of astronomy and science fiction," said Grandpa smoothly, "all that sort of stuff. Please go on."

"Can't get near the thing. Inspector Crope—sensible, keen fella—and two of his men—tried to investigate. But no go. Some kind of force coming from the thing knocked 'em flat. All big fellas, too." He frowned at Robin and said severely, "And don't you say *Gosh* again." He turned to Grandpa. "Must admit though—some brainy creatures running that thing. Thought at first it might be some Communist invasion business. Know definitely now it's not. Thing from outer space all right. And that's why I'm here. Official capacity."

He gave them a stern official-capacity look, daring them to interrupt. Peg saw Robin going bright scarlet, trying to keep his *Goshes* in.

"Here's the situation, all you need to know. Three reliable witnesses—I'm not including Jilks and his man now —saw some creatures—or little machines—that must have come out of the spaceship. Quite definite, all of 'em, on that point."

"But why weren't they invisible, too, Major Rodpath?" James asked.

"Good question, young fella! They *were* invisible— protected by some devilishly clever device—until they were well away from the spaceship. But that's where they came from. No doubt about that. So there are several of these creatures—or machines—or whatever they are— roaming around. Collecting information and reporting back, ten to one. Dam' tricky situation—what?" He looked round for some signs of enthusiastic agreement but didn't get any.

"It's a very unusual situation of course," said Grandpa mildly. "But it needn't be *tricky*—unless we're determined to make it tricky. After all, we're sending space probes to planets simply to collect information."

"Not the same thing at all, Professor. We're not landing enormous spaceships and then making 'em invisible.
Don't know what these creatures may be up to. Taking
no chances, anyhow. Police have been in touch with
nearest military command, naturally. But may be some
time before troops can get here, even if they round up a
helicopter or two. So we're organizing our own drive.
Need everybody who can handle a gun. Even a small
shotgun might help if you can get close enough. What
have you got here?"

"Only an old air gun," said James.

"Useless! One fella said the two creatures he saw
looked armored, but with a powerful gun like mine, I'll
take a chance on that."

Peg couldn't keep quiet any longer. "But you don't
want to *kill* them, do you?"

"Put 'em out of action one way or another. Better
keep out of this, my dear. Men's work. Well, if you
haven't a gun, you haven't. But you lads at least can
keep your eyes open—and be in touch. We're all in a
very dicey situation—must rally round, stand together—
eh?"

Peg thought he must be going now and felt im-
mensely relieved, especially so because James and Robin
had rather drifted away from Snoggle under his rug, not
really covering that corner at all. And then, to her horror,
she saw that Major Rodpath had changed his mind about
going. He was staring and pointing at Snoggle's rug.

"What's going on over there—under that rug?"

Peg made a lightning move to get in front of him and
said very quickly, "Nothing! It's only our old dog—
Snoggle. We were playing a silly game with him—teasing
him—"

The Major moved a little. He looked and sounded very severe. "No way to treat a dog, y'know. And you're half suffocating the poor beast."

James and Robin were now in line with Peg. They were all talking at once.

"You'll frighten him, Major Rodpath—"

"He's a very nervous dog—terribly nervous—"

"He doesn't like strangers, so don't go too near—"

"He absolutely *hates* strangers—"

"Don't—don't—please—he'll bite you." This was Peg almost at the top of her voice. "He really will—*he'll bite you*—"

But this was quite the wrong thing to say. "He won't bite *me*," the Major told her. "I know how to handle a dog. And you obviously don't. Now if you'll get out of my way, I'll show you."

And he was just going to show them, too, when clever Grandpa came to their rescue. He'd gone out, leaving the door open behind him, and now apparently he was standing in the back doorway, shouting to somebody at a distance. "Who?" he was calling. "Major Rodpath . . . ? Yes, he's here. . . . I'll tell him."

The Major had already turned away to listen, and now Grandpa appeared in their doorway. "Somebody seems to want you in a hurry, Major. Couldn't see exactly who it was—my sight's not too good—but I fancy it was a policeman."

"Ten to one you're right. May have spotted something." He picked up his gun. "Chance of using this, I hope." He moved out briskly, but then as he must have reached the back door, they heard him calling back, "And tell those kids to take that dog out of there, Professor."

"I will, Major—I will." Then they could hear Grandpa

closing and bolting the back door. He returned to them smiling. "He's gone."

"*Was* there anybody shouting for him?" James asked.

Grandpa shook his head. He was sitting down now, busy filling his pipe.

"It was just Grandpa's wonderful wizard fab cleverness," cried Peg. "In another minute that horrible beastly man would have discovered Snoggle. And then he would have wanted to shoot him. The horrible, beastly, bloodthirsty man! I'd like to shoot *him*."

"So would I," said Robin.

Grandpa shook his head again but in a different, more serious way. His pipe was alight now, and after a few preliminary puffs he spoke to them, mildly but firmly. "And that's how it all goes on and on, you see. He wants to shoot Snoggle. You want to shoot him. Somebody will then want to shoot *you*. So there's no end to it. So there runs through history a river of blood."

"Oh, Grandpa," Peg began, "I didn't *really* want to shoot him. But you must admit Major Thing's a horror—"

"Not a type I'm fond of, I'll confess," he told her. "But in his own way, he's probably a decent, kind fellow, with a fine sense of duty—and very brave. Ready if necessary to defend Mitchling, Farfield, and Kettleton against monsters with three heads and eight tentacles—"

"Fair enough, Grandpa," said James. "But we've got to keep poor old Snoggle out of his way."

"My goodness—yes!" cried Peg. "And we'll have to *plan* for Snoggle."

"And the first thing to do," James went on, talking as he moved, "is to draw these curtains. We can't have one of these hunting chaps staring in through the window."

It wasn't dark, but it was certainly dim now that the

curtains were drawn. Rather depressing really, Peg thought. She was about to switch the lights on but stopped to listen to Robin, who was talking very earnestly.

"But, Grandpa, why should all these people think the spaceship's come to attack us? All it's done so far is to defend itself—first making itself invisible and then using that force to keep people away. And these strangers, Snoggle's lot—"

"Snogglers," James suggested.

"OK, Snogglers—they're obviously ten times cleverer than we are, but that doesn't mean they've come to *invade* us—or to bother with us at all. They may already think we're a lot of idiots."

"I'm sometimes tempted to agree with them," said Grandpa. "And of course you're right, Robin. These Snogglers may be merely curious, wanting to know a little more about us—"

"But how could they do that," Peg asked, "just sitting there—invisible?"

It was Robin of course who answered her. "Just because they *are* ten times cleverer than we are. They may have ways of finding things out we can't imagine. And another thing, Grandpa. They may not want to be here at all. They may be just breaking a journey—from their planet to another just like it—and have landed here for a halt while they repair something. Snogglers may have landed on earth several times before—50,000 years ago— 100,000 years ago—"

"No, Robin, not now, please!" said Peg. "We have to attend to Snoggle. You and James take his rug off—poor Snoggle!"

Chapter 4

Getting Acquainted

They all looked hard at Snoggle, now free from his rug. He was obviously feeling much better, not drooping at all. His eyes began to move quickly. Then—a great surprise—he took two or three short steps forward. This delighted Peg, who clapped her hands.

"There you are," she cried. "And you're feeling much much better now, aren't you, Snoggle dear? Oh—what a pity we can't talk to you and ask you questions! Where have you come from? Where are you going to?"

This brought Robin in of course. "Gosh—yes! What he could tell us if we could understand him!"

"We must try somehow to make him understand us," said Peg. "He hasn't any ears or a mouth to talk with, but perhaps those four little things on the top of his head will come into it somehow—like wireless—" She ended rather feebly and gave the boys an apologetic look because they understood about wireless and she didn't.

"They're probably some sort of antennae," Grandpa suggested. "But I don't see us ever understanding how they work. However, we ought to keep an eye on them."

"I've been watching them," Robin told him. "But nothing's happened so far. No lighting up—or anything."

"But he does keep giving us such sweet, appealing looks," said Peg. "Don't you, Snoggle darling?"

"Not too much of that soppy stuff, Peg," said Robin. "He's not a kind of egg-shaped spaniel. He's a creature from another planet and probably much cleverer than we are."

"I wonder." This was James, who had a specially good voice for that sort of short pulling-you-up remark.

And as usual, it annoyed Robin. "What d'you mean—you *wonder?* Don't be ridiculous, James. We know now he comes from somewhere among the stars—in a marvelous spaceship—"

"You've missed the point, chump—so keep quiet." James thought a moment, then began slowly, "I like Snoggle—"

"I adore him," cried Peg. "Look at his eyes!"

"Well, that's part of it—in a way—I mean, you adoring him—"

"I feel he's such a pet—"

"But that's just what I mean." James sounded triumphant. "No, shut up, Robin. Listen! Can you see old Snoggle here piloting a spaceship billions and billions of miles? Because I can't."

Nobody spoke for a few moments. How wonderful, Peg thought, if Snoggle could have put in a remark then. But what a hope! And it really was very hard to imagine Snoggle as a super-astronaut.

"In short, James, he is a pet," said Grandpa thoughtfully. "You know, I'm inclined to agree with you. The beings who are responsible for that spaceship, who have made it invisible and are defending it with some mysterious force, beings far in advance of us technologically, belonging to a much older civilization, are probably not like Snoggle at all. Except of course in some particulars, just as we share some things with dogs and cats. Yes, Robin?"

"I think you and James are probably quite right," Robin replied very solemnly. "They brought Snoggle along as we might take a dog."

"You mean, he really *is* a pet?" Peg asked hopefully.

"Yes—and that's why they let him out." But then Robin went on to ruin it. "Unless of course he's really a kind of robot—a little scouting machine—"

"Oh, don't be so stupid!" Peg was furious. "Just look at his beautiful eyes—"

"Doesn't mean a thing. They could be artificial robot eyes—"

"Oh—shut up!" She leaned forward. "They're your eyes, aren't they, Snoggle? But I wish you could talk. Or even make any kind of noise—like barking or purring. Grandpa, can't we teach him something?"

"We can try. Though I don't think communication is going to be easy."

"No—but don't forget," said Robin, "that although he may be only a sort of pet to them, they're so clever and far advanced that Snoggle may soon seem very clever to us."

"What we could truly call an *egghead*. Well, who'll try a few simple words? Peg?"

"All right. But nobody must laugh," she added fiercely. "Snoggle may be very sensitive. And even if he isn't, *I am*. Now then, Snoggle dear. Look at me."

And Snoggle did, but then she had gone rather nearer and pointed at him, catching and fixing his eye. "Girl," said Peg very deliberately, pointing at herself. "*Girl. Girl. Now—Boy.*" She pointed to James. "*Boy.*" At Robin this time. And though she'd been so deliberate, just to make sure she went through the whole thing again, even though she was beginning to feel a bit silly. "Now this time I shan't point. Snoggle—*Boy? Girl? Boy?*"

But Snoggle did nothing, just went on staring at her. "Oh—dear! He's not taking it in, is he? Perhaps he's just stupid."

She knew Robin had been feeling impatient, and now he exploded. "No, it's you who are being stupid, Peg. I knew this *boy* and *girl* thing would be hopeless. It's far too difficult for him, isn't it Grandpa?"

"I'm afraid it is, you know, Peg. You need something more universal. Direction—for instance—"

"Just what I was going to say." Robin was scarlet and bursting with eagerness. "He doesn't understand about boys and girls, but he must understand something about *Up* and *Down*."

"He ought to," said James. "He's been up and up and has come down and down."

"Not funny! Now then, Snoggle—look at me." And Snoggle did because Robin had attracted his attention by moving a hand. Then Robin pointed at the ceiling. "*Up. Up. Up.*" He pointed at the floor. "*Down. Down. Down.*" Then pointing again and looking idiotic, Robin went on, "*Up. Down. Down. Up. Down. Up. Down.* OK—now then, Snoggle—your big chance." He pronounced the words slowly and solemnly several times but without pointing. Snoggle merely looked at him, never up or down.

"A washout if ever I saw one," said James.

"All right, you have a go."

"That's what I'm going to have—A Go. Because I think we need some movement in this lesson." James could be bossy at times, and this was going to be one of them. "You and Peg get over there, and I'll stand by Snoggle. No—further—as far away as possible. OK, that'll do. Now when I shout *Come,* you both march toward me. And when I say *Go,* you turn round and march back. And don't just shamble and slouch. Make it very definite —military style. Ready! *Come!*"

After they had marched up to Snoggle and then back three times, James said, "All right, stand easy—you two. This is where I test Snoggle." He stood in front of Peg and James, staring hard at Snoggle, who seemed to be staring back at him, and then shouted, "*Come. Come.*"

But Snoggle never moved an inch. James was disgusted. "Oh—all right. *Go* then. *Go.*" Nothing happened.

Flopping down on the sofa, Peg felt disheartened. "Oh—it's no use. We can't make him understand *anything.*"

"Perhaps he really is just a kind of robot thing," said Robin, "and has to be switched on."

"I don't believe it," Peg told him. "And I don't believe he's utterly stupid. Look at him! We're making him feel quite miserable. You can say what you like"—she looked round defiantly, even though nobody was saying anything—"but I believe that somehow Snoggle understands *feelings.* He wants to be liked, and if he isn't, then his eyes change, and though he doesn't really droop, being so eggy, somehow he seems to droop. All right, say I'm being silly!" More defiance.

She found an unexpected ally in James. "There's something in this," he said. "I've noticed that his skin—or whatever it is—keeps changing, though you'll probably never spot it unless you're watching it very closely. When he's feeling good, it's brighter. When he's miserable, it gets duller and duller."

53

"Oh—how clever of you, James!" cried Peg. "I'm sure you're right."

"Well, I think you two are overdoing it," said Robin, though not scornfully, quite mildly. "I believe Snoggle might be some kind of machine—a sort of robot scout. Grandpa, what do you think?"

Grandpa waited a moment or two, puffing away, then answered Robin quietly and very deliberately. "I don't think Snoggle's a machine. He's a creature of some kind. And we mustn't conclude he's stupid. It's quite obvious to me—and I've been watching him very carefully—that he can't hear at all, not as we understand hearing. Those antennae things he has on top aren't ears and must have quite a different function—"

Peg had to break in. "One of them tells him what people are *feeling*—"

"Possibly, possibly not. But they certainly belong to some other means of communication we can't hope to understand—"

"Grandpa, I'm sure you're right," cried Robin. "On his planet they don't have sounds—they use something else—"

"And there are times—and more and more of them— when I wish we used something else. I could do with a holiday on a silent planet—"

"But if Snoggle can't hear," said Peg, "he can *see*."

"Yes, he can see—no doubt about that." Grandpa pushed himself out of his chair. "And now we're going to try him out, using sight, not sound. And perhaps—if only to please Peg—some feeling, too. *We must want* Snoggle to join in."

"But join in *what?*" This was James.

"Don't be so impatient, my boy." Grandpa moved toward the door. "Now you three come back here. Then, when I give the signal, march up to Snoggle together, keeping a good rhythm—*left, right—left, right!* When you're close to Snoggle, turn round sharply and march back here, then swing round and march up to him again —and keep going. Not too quickly, mind. About like this —*left, right—left, right!* Now get in line—and keep in line. Ready—go! *Left, right—left, right.*"

Remembering the Snoggle adventure afterward, recalling every bit of it, Peg always thought that this— Grandpa's *march* idea—was easily the best part of it. To begin with, it turned into fun at once, whereas all that solemn testing with words had been hopelessly dreary. Keeping in step and rather banging their feet down, they marched toward Snoggle, turned round—*left, right—left, right*—and went back, marched up to him again, went back, twice, and then three times. But the fourth time they marched up to Snoggle, something tremendous and wonderful happened. As they turned to go back, *Snoggle joined them.* Of course he wasn't very good at marching, his legs being so short, and they had to slow down for him, and even then he couldn't really keep in step. But there he was, with them, playing their game—and enjoying it, too, Peg felt. He was next to her, on the side nearer Grandpa, who was of course just watching, in his place not far from the door. So she couldn't see Snoggle's eyes, though she was sure they were flashing away, but, looking down, it did seem to her that one of the antenna things, just one out of the four, was almost beginning to glow. And she was so happy, she risked giving him a pat on the back—if you could call it his back—and it felt like patting a tinny crocodile.

"We've communicated, Grandpa," James shouted.

"I know, I know. Keep going a little longer."

"We're the first people ever to do it with somebody from outer space," Robin cried breathlessly. "Good old Snoggle! Don't weaken, big boy!"

"He may be tiring a bit, though," said Peg, still on the march. "He must be so heavy—and his legs are so short—poor duck!"

They had turned round for the fifth time since Snoggle had joined them when Grandpa shouted, "Stop! Stop! The curtains don't quite meet now, and I saw somebody looking through the window. See who it was, one of you!"

Robin just beat Peg, and the gap was small, so that only one could look. In two seconds Robin was turning back to them and saying, "It was that Mrs. Bing-Birchall. She's hurrying across the lawn now."

"To spread the news," said James, disgusted. "We'll have to put Snoggle under that rug again until we decide what to do."

"Oh—no," cried Peg, looking at poor Snoggle who was now standing in the middle of the room, wondering no doubt why the game had stopped. "He'll feel so disappointed and miserable."

"Oh—yes," said James in one of his grim tones. "He'll feel a lot worse if Mrs. Bing-Bang and Co. nab him. Come on, Robin, give me a hand with him."

Peg wanted to cry but wouldn't allow herself to, this being such an emergency. She blinked hard as she went to Grandpa, turning her back on the boys and Snoggle. "If she saw him, Grandpa, what are we going to do now?"

"Find him a good hiding place, I imagine, my dear. But let's wait for James and Robin, who may have some good ideas. But you can start thinking. You know the house better than I do."

But Peg found she simply didn't want to think about putting Snoggle in some remote cupboard. And of course as soon as James and Robin joined them, it was worse.

"Well, what do we do with Snoggle now?" James began in a horrid businessman voice. "Take him up to one of the attics?"

"We could empty one of those old trunks in the box room," Robin suggested. "Leave the lid open a bit to allow him some air."

"And pile a lot of stuff round the trunk," said James, "to discourage anybody who's searching."

"You don't know there'll be anybody searching," cried Peg, who now hated all this. "I think it's a rotten, horrible idea."

"But we can't leave him under that rug, my dear," Grandpa told her gently. "If the Major comes here again, he'll make straight for that rug, greatly annoyed because we fooled him last time."

"Of course," said James. "Obviously the rug's out. And you'd better keep out of this, Peg. Cool, calm judgment needed here, girl."

"Oh—fiddle-faddle! I ought to be in it more than you. I'm the sorriest for poor Snoggle. And I'm *thinking* about him harder than you are. Not as something to be stuffed away—but as a sort of person."

"Peg has a point there, James," Grandpa told him. "And in the end she may be wiser than we are. However, something'll have to be done—fairly soon, too."

"I'm not sure about that," Robin announced to all three of them. "I know I said Mrs. Bing-Birchall was hurrying across the lawn. But I meant *hurrying* for her— and she's no fast mover. And she might have several big fields to cross before she finds anybody to listen to her. Still, we must decide what to do."

"And that's quite obvious." James was now in one of his big, bossy moods. "We hide him somewhere upstairs, the higher, the better. Robin—you find a few possible places, starting with the box room, I'd say—while Grandpa, Peg, and I handle Snoggle."

"Can do," said Robin and darted off.

"I hate this," Peg cried. "I hate it. I hate it. And it won't be any use—you'll see."

Chapter 5

All Wrong

It was quite a business taking Snoggle out of the room and then along the hall to the bottom of the stairs. The three of them had to do a lot of pushing and half carrying, and Snoggle seemed to get heavier every minute. Even before they reached the stairs, Peg's arms ached, Grandpa did some groaning, and James was becoming impatient.

"This is far worse than bringing him in from outside," James told them. "It's like handling a huge bag of lead."

Peg said nothing to the others, but she began to wonder if Snoggle could make himself heavier and heavier. She was sure now that he didn't want to go where they were taking him, perhaps to be left by himself, with nobody to look at and no more marching games. Somehow he *knew*, just as Peg did, that this idea was all wrong, and he showed he was against it by working this heavier-and-heavier trick. And if she believed this, she thought, then it was silly to keep on straining and pushing and lifting until her arms ached. She didn't want Grandpa to do too much, but James was a strong boy and it was he who'd insisted that Snoggle should go upstairs. So let James struggle away until he had armache and backache.

All Wrong

By the time they arrived at the bottom of the stairs—poor Snoggle standing there, with his eyes closed now—even James said they ought to have a rest.

"Tell you what I'm going to do," James told them, after taking a few deep breaths, "as soon as Snoggle's safely hidden away. First, I'm going to mend the front doorbell. That's easy—I've done it before. Then I'll put a notice on the back door telling people they must go round to the front. Get the idea?"

Grandpa and Peg said they didn't.

"Well, I'm assuming now that we're still in the playroom—not you, Grandpa—you may be in your room working—"

"You're paying a great compliment to my powers of concentration, James. I must say I don't see myself doing any work in this peculiar atmosphere—spaceship creature hidden away, people coming with guns—but go on."

"It'll give us far more time to prepare ourselves and take any necessary action," said James rather grandly. "Back door no good. They must go round and ring the front doorbell. One of us answers it. All taking time and giving us time. Now d'you see?"

Grandpa promptly replied that he did and that James was being very clever. Peg said nothing, because something important had now occurred to her, but this didn't seem the moment to tell them.

"The trouble about getting this chap upstairs," said Grandpa, looking doubtfully at Snoggle, "is that being such an eggy type, he's got nothing like arms to help him. We'll have to lift him stair by stair, and that's not going to be easy. Is it only my imagination—or is he really getting heavier and heavier the more we move him?"

"He can't be," James replied, "though I know how you

feel. But we're just imagining it. What's the matter with you, Peg?"

"I think he hates this, just as I do, and so he really *is* making himself heavier and heavier."

"Oh—come off it!" James was very scornful. "How could he? Be sensible."

"What's the use of telling me to be sensible? Or asking me how he could make himself heavier?" Peg was almost shouting. "What's a spaceship doing here—invisible, too? Who brought Snoggle here and then let him out to explore? What's sensible about all of this?"

"Good point, Peg," said Grandpa.

"The only thing that *is* sensible is Snoggle," she continued hotly. "He's a very strange shape—and we don't know what he can do and what he can't do—but he's friendly and really rather sweet—and he's depending on us. Look at him—he's giving us one of his very appealing looks—poor Snoggle!" And he was, too, though he didn't keep his eyes open for long. She began to wonder if he wasn't feeling exhausted again.

Ignoring Peg's outburst, James became the man-in-charge once more. "I may be wrong, but I thought I heard Robin calling down. After all, we haven't so much time to waste. So let's hoist Snoggle up the stairs. And I must say I agree with Grandpa. I wish Snoggle had something like arms or paws or claws to help him—and us. OK then—up with him!"

As soon as Snoggle faced the bottom step, Peg felt sure he had never seen anything like it before. Either everything was on one floor on his planet, or they'd used nothing but elevators for thousands and thousands of years—or of course the things in the subway and some big shops—escalators. She could imagine Snoggle, with his large flat feet or paws, moving easily up and down on escalators. Perhaps he was waiting—because he obviously didn't want to move—for the Hooper staircase to turn itself into an escalator. She tried to say something like this to James, but he was now too impatient to listen.

"Oh—*come on!*" he cried, just as if Snoggle could hear him. "Look we'll have to lift as well as push—and first really get down to it."

"Not me, my boy," said Grandpa. "Otherwise, you and Peg will have to lift me up, too. I'll go up a step or two and try to pull him."

These stairs were broad and not very high, but even so, James nearly burst himself getting Snoggle up the first two of them. What made it worse was that Snoggle didn't seem to be able to adjust his feet or paws properly and slipped and slithered about. But then Peg knew very well that he wasn't really trying because he was *against it.* Just as she was, so that she merely looked as if she were helping James. And even when they had only reached the second step, he found her out.

"Peg Hooper"—giving her a terribly accusing look— "you're not trying at all. You're just pretending to help. You're a complete fraud." He stopped there, being almost out of breath and wanting to mop his face.

"Come, come, James," said Grandpa. "I'm sure Peg's doing her best."

"I'm sorry, Grandpa, but she isn't, while I'm half killing myself. And we've hardly started yet. Honestly she's useless—just in the way. She pretends to be so desperately attached to poor old Snoggle—"

"Oh—shut up!" Peg felt she either had to shout or begin bawling, hurrying away in tears, so she decided to shout and shout. "It's because I know this idiotic stairs thing is useless, useless, useless—and all wrong—and I know that Snoggle thinks so, too—"

"Don't be so utterly daft, girl," James yelled at her. "You don't know what Snoggle thinks. You don't know if he thinks at all. He may be just a sort of machine as Robin says—"

"He isn't—he isn't—he isn't. I *know* he isn't."

"Oh—turn it up! You don't know anything—"

"Now, stop this, you two," Grandpa told them, rather sternly for him.

"All right, Grandpa. No more shouting." Peg hesitated a moment. Then, "But if Robin and James think he may be just a machine, why are they worrying about somebody shooting him?"

"And that, my boy," said Grandpa, twinkling now, "is an excellent example of the deadly feminine thrust, right under your guard. But if you want to go on with this, I suggest that Peg runs upstairs and sends Robin down."

"Dead right, Grandpa! Robin and I can manage him. Pop off, Peg. Tell Robin it's *Mayday* and *SOS*."

She found Robin at the bottom of the stairs that went to the top of the house. She gave him James's message. "OK! I've found a jolly good empty trunk at the far end of the box room. But I can't help wondering about these stairs, Peg. They're a lot steeper and narrower than the other stairs. What d'you think?"

"I'll tell you what I think," she began fiercely. "I think you and James are behaving like a pair of loonies. We've only got Snoggle up two steps so far, and even if you help James, it's going to take ages. As for those steps up to the attic, you'd have to carry Snoggle every inch of the way. And if you think you can do that, I must warn you that I believe Snoggle's deliberately making himself heavier and heavier. Just because he's *against it*—like me."

"Heavier and heavier?" Robin laughed. "Now that's really round the bend. Not possible."

"Well, that's the last thing I'd expect you to say, Robin Hooper. James, yes, but not you—with all your galaxies and White Dwarfs and spaceships! Not possible? Why—Snoggle wouldn't have been possible this morning. You're talking just like Major Thing and Mrs. Bing-Bang."

"Jolly good, Peg!" He said it quite admiringly. This was one very good thing about Robin, though of course he could be irritating in other ways: he would freely admit he'd been wrong. "Yes, of course it's possible—for a creature from another planet. But I'd have to judge for myself that he's getting heavier and heavier."

"You'll soon be able to do that. Listen—James is shouting for you. And tell him these attic stairs are absolutely hopeless. He won't believe me."

"OK." Robin moved off, to join the others below, but called over his shoulder, "Perhaps we could bring the trunk down—and then carry him up in it."

"Never, never, never!" she screamed after him. "The whole idea's wrong."

Now she went up the attic stairs herself, not to go into the box room and look at that horrible trunk, but to find the best window with a view over the fields, to see if any enemies were approaching. But there was nobody in sight, not a single person, and this was comforting because it meant they would have more time to find the right place for Snoggle. And already she was rehearsing arguments to prove it would be safest if he stayed with them somewhere in the playroom.

When she returned to the floor below, she found Grandpa at the top of the stairs. Snoggle and the boys were only about halfway up. They were puffing and sweating, and it seemed to her that Snoggle himself, with his eyes closed at that moment, looked as bad as he had when he first arrived in the house.

"I've been given the sack," said Grandpa. "James says they can do better without me. And I don't say he's wrong."

"Well, I say the whole idea's wrong," she replied fiercely. "And Snoggle's just as much against it as I am. If he'd been for it, as he was for our marching game, he'd have been up here long since. I'm not saying he's a good stair-climber—they probably don't have any stairs where he lives—but he'd have managed somehow. But, Grandpa, I'm sure he *knows,* just as I do, that this whole thing about hiding him upstairs is ridiculous. Even if we could get him into that trunk in the box room, I think he might die just because he'd be so miserable. Don't you see?"

"Not quite," said Grandpa thoughtfully. "I've always assumed that one of us would have to stay up there with him."

"But then if somebody was searching the house for Snoggle—and if we don't believe that can happen, then why are we bothering at all?—and that somebody found one of us sitting in the box room staring at an old trunk, then we'd have had it, Grandpa. Good-bye, Snoggle! If we left him alone, we wouldn't know what was happening—and I'd feel so anxious, I'd be more than half dotty. No, please, Grandpa, let me finish. I've worked out the whole argument. Now if nobody's coming to search the house, then what's the use of James and Robin getting blue in the face trying to move Snoggle upstairs, and —what's worse—poor Snoggle himself feeling miserable and terribly exhausted? Now if you agree—"

"It's a negative argument, Peg, but so far I agree with it—"

"Why a negative argument?"

"Because you're saying what mustn't be done with Snoggle, but not what *must* be done with him—"

"I'm coming to that, Grandpa." She glanced down and saw that Snoggle had been pushed up another step, though he seemed to be swaying a bit. "The point is, you must back me up. Robin'll be all right. It's James. He won't listen to me just because I'm two years younger— and a girl. Oh—look!"

Snoggle was toppling back, and the boys were desperately trying to hold him so that he didn't go rolling all the way down. Peg was there in a flash, with Grandpa lumbering behind, and the four of them working together managed to bring Snoggle upright again on the step. But they had to hold him to keep him steady there. After a moment, he opened one eye—something Peg had never seen him do before—and it seemed to her that he gave her a piteous, appealing look.

This touched off Peg as if she were a firework. "I don't care what anybody says—or does—but I'm not going to have any more of this. It's *out*. Snoggle isn't going to be pushed up another single step. The idea won't work, and anyhow I knew from the first it was all wrong. So now we pack it up."

"Who says so?" This was James of course.

"I say so," cried Peg, loud and clear. "And Grandpa says so. And I'll bet Robin does really."

"I'll admit we can't get him up those attic stairs." Robin looked at James. "If you don't believe me, go and see for yourself."

James was still resisting her, out of sheer obstinacy. "Grandpa," he asked, quite politely, "are you on Peg's side in this?"

Grandpa nodded. "She has some good arguments against this hiding-upstairs plan. I must say, she's convinced me. But she's not told me yet what her alternative is."

"Perhaps she hasn't one."

"Oh yes, I have," Peg declared boldly. "And it's the only sensible thing we can do."

But it was at that moment that they heard a loud, insistent knocking on the front door.

"Do we leave it—or not," James whispered.

"Better to answer it, I think," said Grandpa very quietly. "I'll go. Push Snoggle to one side, so that I can squeeze past."

Knock. Knock. Knock, knock, knock.

"Whoever it is mustn't come in, Grandpa," Peg hissed at him. "Snoggle can be seen from just inside the door."

"I'm quite aware of that, my dear," Grandpa murmured as he squeezed past Snoggle. "But you three take care—and be quiet." Then he fairly trotted down the last few steps and along the hall. He opened the door only a few inches and kept his hand on it. "Sorry, Constable—" *Constable, eh?* "But I was upstairs. Anything I can do for you?"

He must be an oldish policeman because he had a deep rumble of a voice. "And I'm sorry to disturb you, sir, but I have a message for Inspector Crope. Is he here?"

"No, he isn't. Ought he to be? I'm afraid I don't know anything about an Inspector Crope."

"Quite understand, sir. But when I was given the message, I was told he might be along here. I notice you have a telephone, sir. Would you mind if I put through a call to our Mitchling station?"

"Sorry again—but our telephone's not been working for the last three days. Something's gone wrong with the line outside, they say—and they've mislaid the plan of our local lines. Great nuisance!"

"Always is, sir—yes. Well, I'll be on my way."

It was then that Grandpa proved to Peg that you can be old and yet bold at the same time. "Wish I could help you, Constable. By the way, is there any particular reason why Inspector—what is it?—Crope might be along here?"

The policeman's rumble went deeper, but Peg could still hear him. "It's this queer spaceship business, sir."

"Oh that—yes indeed. Major Rodpath said something about a spaceship—"

"I fancy Major Rodpath is helping Inspector Crope, sir. They say some rum creatures have gotten out of this spaceship—"

"Good gracious me! Can it be true?" Oh—the cool cheek of Grandpa!

"Well, all I know for certain, sir, is that Inspector Crope has been put in charge of rounding 'em up. And if it can be done, the Inspector's the man to do it. Well—good afternoon, sir!"

"Good afternoon, Constable!" And Grandpa waited a moment or two, then quietly closed and locked the door. He came to the foot of the stairs, relit his pipe as he looked up at them, twinkling away, and said, "Well, now we know. Inspector Crope next."

"Yes," said Robin, "and he's not silly, like Major Rodpath."

"They say," James added rather gloomily, "he's very hot stuff."

Chapter 6

Master Plan (Tea Included)

"Well, now I'll tell you my plan," Peg announced. "But first we must put poor Snoggle back in the playroom —where he's longing to be."

James of course had to make a last stand. "How d'you know he is?"

"I'll bet you anything. You'll see—he'll be quite different going back there."

"I'll believe it when I see it," James told her. "And anyhow, don't tell me you're thinking of working that dog-under-the-rug trick again. If this Crope does come here, he'd spot it in half a second."

"Oh—do stop making objections, James! We're only wasting time. Snoggle only goes back under the rug for a while. That's not the idea—though the playroom is. Now, Snoggle my pet—we'll have to turn you round somehow so that you're facing the right way."

Snoggle may or may not have helped instead of hindering them when they took him back to the playroom, but there was no doubt at all, as Peg pointed out triumphantly, that it was very much easier than trying to take him upstairs.

In two or three minutes they were back in their room

—and Snoggle's—and used the same rug again to cover him.

"Only temporary of course," said Peg. "And it'll give him a chance to recover. Where he's really going to be hidden is in this cupboard."

"So that's the idea—the cupboard," said James, looking and sounding rather disgusted. "Well, I'm dead against it—"

"But give Peg a chance to explain," Grandpa told him.

"First, we clear out all our old junk. Or at least most of it," she went on. "Now I remember there's a rod for hanging things on, about a third of the way inside. So we collect all the macs and raincoats and overcoats we can find—and a lot of hangers of course—and then we hide Snoggle behind them. There'll be room for him. We can even leave the cupboard doors open then. Nothing to see but raincoats."

She looked inquiringly at Grandpa and Robin—she wasn't risking James yet—and they nodded their approval.

"Now this means we're in our own room if anybody comes," Peg continued, "and not lurking suspiciously up in the box room or down in the cellar. We can keep an eye on Snoggle instead of wondering what's happening to him. And I don't care what anybody says, this is easily the best way to hide Snoggle."

"Agreed," said Grandpa. "James?"

"I'm doubtful—and it's going to be an awful sweat taking all our stuff out—but I'll admit I haven't a better idea."

"OK, so let's get cracking," cried Robin. "Bang on, Peg!"

"And while you're clearing the cupboard," Grandpa

told them, "I'll begin collecting raincoats and hangers. We must hurry this up, you know."

"And don't forget I'll have to mend the front doorbell," said James. "*And* do a couple of notices."

Grandpa had gone, and now the three of them were starting to empty the cupboard. "But what are we going to do with all this muck?" asked Robin.

But Peg had worked that out, too. "We bung it into that dark cupboardy place under the stairs. Nothing much there. And let's take big armfuls."

"All right," said James. "But I'll have to turn it up soon—to get on with my bell-and-notice work."

Shortly afterwards he left them, and then Grandpa came back with a lot of coats and hangers, dumped them near the cupboard, and went off for more. Peg took a breather between rushes from the cupboard to the place under the stairs and had a quick peep at Snoggle under his rug. He seemed to give her a good lively look and was obviously feeling much better than he'd been on the stairs. Robin worked harder but never stopped babbling about spaceships and remote strange planets, even though Peg wasn't really listening to him. Grandpa came back with a second lot of raincoats and hangers, told them they had enough now, and waited until they'd stopped diving into the cupboard so that he could begin hanging the screen of coats.

When the cupboard was more or less empty and two-thirds of it was completely hidden behind the coats, Grandpa sat down, looking rather weary, and said, "I'll tell you one thing. I'd welcome a cup of tea. Whose turn is it today?"

"It's mine," Peg replied. "And I'll get it ready in a

minute. But first we must put Snoggle into the cupboard and hide that rug."

"OK!" said Robin. "But I'll tell you another thing, Grandpa. I've been thinking about this. Drawing those curtains wasn't a good idea. To begin with, it looks suspicious, because it's still daylight. To go on with—we can't see if anybody's coming. And we could see them much quicker than they could see us in here. So I say—no curtains."

"I believe Robin's right, Grandpa," said Peg. "Don't you? Right then—but we must move Snoggle first. Come on!"

She felt that Snoggle was delighted to escape from the rug, but then he probably thought there was to be another marching game. Certainly he wasn't keen on going into the cupboard, and they had to push him in. Then he had to be pushed back behind the screen of coats. "But if there's nobody strange about, Snoggle darling," she said to him, "you can always come forward a bit—and peep out—like this." And she made an opening in the coats for him. "You can do that for yourself, can't you? That's it! Clever, clever Snoggle!"

"What's the use of that special soppy voice and calling him *Clever, clever Snoggle* and *Darling*," said Robin, "when you know very well he can't hear a thing? Idiotic, I call it."

"Well, you're wrong," Peg replied confidently. "He may not be able to hear as we do, but I'm absolutely sure he understands feelings. Perhaps one of those things on the top does it. So it's not silly to talk to him lovingly. Talking like that makes me feel loving toward him. And he understands what I'm feeling—he really does."

"I'm inclined to agree with that, Robin," said Grandpa in his rather slow, careful way. "There seems to me a distinct possibility—"

But there he stopped because they could hear the front doorbell ringing, though in a distant, jerky sort of way.

Peg cried in alarm, "Oh—there's somebody there—"

"No, there isn't," said Robin. "It's just James trying the bell." He went out, leaving the door open behind him, and after the bell rang again, much louder and steadier this time, Peg heard him shouting along the hall. "Turn it up, James! We know you've mended the bell. And so what?"

Robin came back and began to pull the curtains apart. James arrived, looking pleased with himself. "It's my opinion," he began, "that anybody who shouts *So what?* is stupid. Now I'll explain what I've done. The front doorbell's mended, as you've just heard. And now on the door is a notice that says *Please Ring Bell*. And on the back door is a notice: *Please Go Round to Front Door*. So if any Snoggle-hunters come along, we won't be taken by surprise—we'll have a little warning."

Peg smiled at him. "James, I think that's *very clever*. And I hope you agree it's better not to keep the curtains drawn, so that we can see in good time if anybody's coming this way. Here—I'll switch the light off now. And if you and Robin will tidy up a bit in here—and keep an eye on Snoggle, who may want to come out of the cupboard—I'll get tea ready."

"Scones for me if we have any," said James. "And steady, Peg, don't overdo the Little Mother act. We're not doing *Peter Pan*."

"And that's something to be thankful for," said Robin.

"Scones for me, too, Peg, but not that loathsome plum jam again."

In the kitchen, which luckily was quite big in the Hoopers' house, Peg had put cups, saucers, plates, and knives on the trolley, had filled the large kettle and had lit the gas under it, and was now busy buttering scones when Grandpa drifted in. "Thought you might like me to give you a hand."

She was glad to see him, even though, in fact, she managed better when he didn't give her a hand. At least they could talk seriously without the boys chiming in, making silly jokes. She often had cozy talks with Grandpa, and though this was anything but a cozy day, together they might be able to make it seem a little cozier.

"Has poor Snoggle tried to get out of his cupboard yet?" she asked.

"Just once—and the boys had to push him back. He turned on his miserable look."

"He might have been missing me," Peg said rather proudly. "Honestly, Grandpa, I'm sure he recognizes me. He knows I have more feeling for him than you and the boys have. Will you look in that tin, please, and see if there's any of that sticky dark cake left?"

"Well," said Grandpa slowly, after bringing out the cake, "take care you're not too attached to Snoggle. Just remember, my dear, that even if we rescue him from the Inspector Cropes and Major Rodpaths and Mrs. Bing-Bangs, he'll have to leave us soon."

"I've been trying not to think about that—"

"Impossible to keep him here, Peg. We could never begin to look after him properly. Even the very air isn't right for him. We can't imagine how he's fed. Besides, if you feel he's really an affectionate creature—"

"And I do, Grandpa, I do. Even though he's such a weird shape, he's a *born pet*—"

"Then he'd soon miss his masters—and God knows what they're like—and his playmates and be wretchedly homesick."

"I know, I know, I know. Even if we save him, he must go back to his spaceship. And how are we going to manage that?"

"So far, I haven't the least notion," Grandpa confessed. "That's Problem Two. We're still facing Problem One—to keep him safe—"

"Then what if the spaceship went without him?" Peg almost wailed it. "Leaving him billions and billions and billions of miles behind. I don't think I like this Space Age, Grandpa."

"I'm certain I don't. Unlike Robin, for instance, I hate even reading about it. I fancy I'd have been happier when men seemed to live on a flat solid earth, with a blue dome of sky above it, and heaven somewhere just beyond that."

"Me, too. Oh—look at the kettle! No, I'll do it, but there's not going to be any warming-the-pot fancy work."

Two minutes later, Grandpa was carrying the big teapot and a jug of hot water while Peg wheeled the trolley into the playroom. Nobody said much at first when cups were being filled and scones and jam were being passed around. The cupboard doors were open, but Snoggle was not visible behind his screen of macs and raincoats. Even Peg, busy with the tea things, felt for a few moments that it was just like teatime on an ordinary sort of day.

But then Robin, talking with his mouth full, started it again. "Y'know, Grandpa, I've been thinking about Snoggle—and the spaceship people. If you can call them people—"

"More convenient to call them people," Grandpa told him. "More sensible, too, even though they may have three heads—or no bodies at all—"

"Oh—look at Snoggle!" cried Peg. He was coming slowly out of the cupboard, his huge eyes blazing away.

Robin went into action at once. "Come on, James. Whoa, steady, Snoggle boy! Can't come out just yet." And he and James went nearer and made pushing motions with their hands, never actually touching Snoggle, who with tiny backward steps slowly retreated into the cupboard.

However, he remained just inside it, not retiring behind the screen of macs and raincoats. Peg, who was watching closely, noticed that the darkish-green fire died out of his eyes, and she was almost certain that he knew she was there and that he gave her a reproachful look.

"Obviously," Grandpa said to the boys, "he understands your *Stop—Go* signals. It may be very elementary communication, but it's there all right."

"We tried it while you were in the kitchen," James announced, "and we saw that it worked."

"Y'know, perhaps he can read our thoughts," Robin began.

Peg had to cut in here. "I'll bet anything he understands our feelings—"

"All right, Peg," Robin continued. "Let's agree that he understands our feelings toward him, that he *knows* we're friendly. Grandpa?"

"Very well, my boy. We'll take it that he does. Go on."

Master Plan (Tea Included)

Robin looked very solemn. "This is what's worrying me about the spaceship people. We've already agreed they must be much cleverer than Snoggle. What he can do, they can do better—"

"Sorry to break in, Robin," said Grandpa, "but that doesn't necessarily follow. For example, we have dogs that can follow scents for miles, something quite impossible for us to do. However, you've a point to make. What is it?"

"Let's suppose the spaceship people came here feeling quite friendly. To make a little Earth report perhaps— maybe to test our atmosphere. Or not bothering about us at all. Landing their spaceship to repair something. Ready to take off again when they've done the job. That's *possible*, isn't it?" He looked round for support. Peg was pouring out more tea; Grandpa was filling his pipe; James was halfway through a huge slice of cake; but at least none of them contradicted him.

"They may have landed here before—but ages ago and perhaps in the middle of Siberia or the Pacific Ocean, where nobody ever saw them—"

"Get on with it, Robin," James told him. "We've had all this before. Come to the point, Mastermind."

"Suppose these spaceship people can read thoughts or understand feelings," Robin went on, "and now they're surrounded by types like Mrs. Bing-Bang and Major Rodpath and this Inspector Crope, all waiting to take a crack at them—then what are *they* going to think? If we've turned nasty, they may turn nasty. Then what? Why, they could probably wipe out the whole county in a couple of seconds."

Peg wasn't having this. "I don't see why they should. Do you, Grandpa?"

"Seems to me very unlikely. Look what's happened. By some device they've made their spaceship invisible to us. At the same time they've used some force, like a wall of electricity, to keep people away. But that's all. They're only protecting themselves."

"But they aren't protecting Snoggle, are they?" said Robin, with a rather sinister emphasis.

The silence that followed was broken by Peg. "We don't *know* they aren't," she cried hopefully. "It may be all right really and we may be worrying about nothing." She looked round, and what she saw made her come to an end feebly with, "Don't you think?"

"Well, I don't for one," said James.

Then Robin had to come up with one of his horrible science-fiction ideas. "But then perhaps they don't care what happens to Snoggle. Perhaps they've only to touch a switch or press a button to make dozens of Snoggles in a few minutes—"

"Stop it, stop it, Robin!" cried Peg. "Snoggle isn't a machine thing at all. Just look at him! Waiting so patiently. I wish we could give him some cake. You're a good clever Snoggle, aren't you? But I wish you didn't seem to have so little of everything—no mouth, no ears, no nose—"

"But he's got those antennae things on the top of his head," said Robin. "And they may be very elaborate arrangements—"

"Quite so," said Grandpa. "For all we know, he may be receiving messages from the spaceship at this very moment—"

"Gosh—yes!"

"Well, if he is—" and then James held up a hand warningly and said the rest in what was nearly down to a whisper—"I hope they're telling him we've got some people at the back door." He crept out to listen, not closing the playroom door behind him.

Peg saw no point in keeping quiet, so, for the benefit of anybody listening outside, she asked in a loud, clear, and actressy tone, "Would anybody like any more of this delicious cake?" At the same time she pointed urgently at the cupboard.

"I'd like another cup of tea, my dear," said Grandpa, but like a man in a play.

James came back. "I think they've gone round to the front door now. So my little wheeze has worked. So let's make sure Snoggle's safely behind the coats. Because if somebody opens the cupboard doors and there he is, staring them in the face, we've all had it." So he and Robin gently pushed Snoggle behind the coats and then closed the cupboard doors, while Peg gave Grandpa another cup of tea.

"Thank you, my dear. Mind you, we don't know these people are looking for Snoggle. They may be selling onions—or something."

"No, Grandpa," Peg told him quite firmly. "They're Snoggle-hunters. I *know* they are. Oh—Robin—what are you doing?"

"What d'you think? Locking the cupboard doors of course. And bags I the key."

"Well, I don't think that's very clever—"

"You don't want us to leave the doors open, do you?" James sounded horrified.

"That's what I'd do. I know it would mean depending entirely on the coats to hide Snoggle," Peg continued. "But I'd risk that, just because if the cupboard doors were open, nobody'd be suspicious—"

"That's being *too* clever—"

But now they could hear the front doorbell. "I'll go," said Grandpa. "And if they're the Snoggle-hunters, I'll try to give you some warning signal before I actually bring them in here. Steady now! No loud arguments about the cupboard doors! *Alert's* on."

Chapter 7

More Air but Hot Work

Grandpa gave them the warning he'd promised them, because they could hear him speaking in a loud-actor false voice as he led the way to their room. "I've just been taking tea with the youngsters. I usually do, in their play-room." And as soon as Peg and the boys heard this, they made warning faces at one another and hurriedly put cups and plates back on the trolley.

Then, as Peg said afterwards, it was just as if they were invaded by an army. The room seemed full of large strange bodies and guns. Robin started to giggle and had to turn away and pretend to blow his nose. Major Rod-path, carrying the same shotgun, didn't look any differ-ent, but Mrs. Bing-Birchall, also with gun, was now wear-ing an enormous slouch hat and some sort of tweed cape. For all the space they seemed to take up, there was only one other person, and now Grandpa was introducing them to him or him to them.

"My grandchildren—Peg, James, and Robin Hooper—Inspector Crope."

They didn't get a smile from the Inspector—just a hard look each. He had a square face and one of those old-fashioned moustaches, bigger than Major Rodpath's but tidier, not a chewed one. He was a new type to Peg, who liked to notice people, because while he was one of those large wooden men, common enough, she knew at once that unlike most of them he wasn't stupid. They usually had dimmish eyes, and his were small, bright, quick, as if a cunning little animal were looking out of that big wooden face. He wore a superior kind of police uniform and had his right arm through the strap of a rifle. She thought he must have fought in some war or wars because he was wearing several of those colored ribbons that generals wear by the dozen. She didn't like the look of him at all. This wasn't another Major Rodpath. She hoped the boys were telling themselves they'd have to be very careful now.

Major Rodpath did a little preliminary barking. "Back again—you youngsters, eh what? But this time Inspector Crope's in charge. Advise you not to talk any nonsense to *him*. Wouldn't work at all. Not a hope. You'd know that if you'd heard him give as much evidence in court as I have. So—*watch it!* Take over, Inspector."

But Mrs. Bing-Birchall didn't give him a chance. "Just a moment," she began, shouting away. "It really is dreadfully, dreadfully stuffy in here. I don't know how you can possibly bear it."

"We like it stuffy," said Peg.

"Nonsense! Youngsters your age need plenty of good fresh air—"

Somehow Grandpa managed to cut in, though he sounded like an apologetic mouse after Mrs. Bing-Bang's stern bellowing. "I'm afraid it's my fault, Mrs. Bing-Birchall. There seemed to be rather an unpleasant draft when those wide French windows were open."

She didn't shout *Nonsense* at him, but before replying she closed her eyes and then opened them enormously, as if Grandpa oughtn't to be still there when she looked a second time. "Professor Hooper, I've been out and about for the last hour—and there's hardly a breath of wind. In fact, as it's been a thundery August day, it's *close*— decidedly close. And as we all have to keep our wits about us—that's true, isn't it, Inspector?"

"It would help—certainly, madam."

"Then for goodness' sake, everybody, let's have some decent fresh air in this room." She made a move toward the windows, but the Inspector, surprisingly quick for a large wooden man, forestalled her.

"Let me do it, Mrs. Bing-Birchall." But when he got to the windows, he stopped and turned, looked chiefly at James, and said in what seemed to Peg a very sinister tone, "Unless of course you've some particular and peculiar reason for keeping these windows tight shut. *And* stuffing paper round them."

"Well-yes-well," James began slowly. And then couldn't go on, probably catching a warning glance from Grandpa.

"Well what, young man?" the Inspector demanded.

"Just going to say—I stuffed those cracks with paper when it started raining so hard—you know, the thunderstorm."

"So now that it's not raining—or likely to rain very soon," said the Inspector, still making it sinister, "you can take all that paper out while I open the windows. Right?"

Poor James daren't refuse and hastily began on the paper while the Inspector opened the windows as wide as they would go.

Mrs. Bing-Bang, to Peg's disgust, did some triumphant sniffing. "Ah—that's better—*much* better. Now we can breathe. Nothing like good fresh air!"

Peg muttered, "Oh—rats!" and began moving the crockery around on the trolley just to make a noise.

"Mustn't waste too much time," said the Major at the top of his bark. "Take over, Inspector."

"I'll do that, sir," he shouted, "as soon as this young lady stops making so much noise."

Peg could shout, too, and now she did. "I'm trying to get these tea things out of the room. Then you'll have more space for all your guns."

"And I think you're being impertinent," Mrs. Bing-Birchall shouted. But Peg was already pushing the trolley out of the room. When she hurriedly returned, she found that Inspector Crope had taken a commanding position not far from the windows and was beginning a speech, chiefly addressed to Grandpa.

"I believe you understand about the spaceship, sir," he said in a very official I'm-telling-you tone, "and about some of the creatures from it roaming around. The military ought to be taking over soon, but in the meantime we've been given instructions—very *special* instructions— to round up and—if necessary—destroy these creatures."

"You have?" said Grandpa. "I wonder why."

The Inspector went on as if Grandpa had never spoken. "As you probably know, sir, we're not an armed force. It's only on very rare occasions we're allowed to carry arms, though most of us have had some training in the use of them." As he swung the rifle round, he looked at the boys and Peg. "So if I show you this rifle, it's just to make you all understand that this is a very serious business. We're not playing games. May be a matter of life and death."

Peg wondered whose life and death it was going to be a matter of, but didn't say anything. She tried staring in a scornful way at this Crope, only to discover that he was a much better starer than she was. Also, it concentrated his attention on her.

"And now I'd like to ask you a question or two," Crope continued, hardly giving the boys a glance, staring away at her. "From information received, I gather that about half an hour ago you three young people were seen marching up and down this room—*with a creature.*"

"I distinctly saw it," Mrs. Bing-Bang shouted. "A most *extraordinary* creature."

"Quite so," said the Inspector. "A most extraordinary creature. Well?"

Her mind working fast, Peg decided that all she could do was to laugh this off. So she started laughing, and though it didn't sound quite real, she did her best. After a moment or two, James and Robin joined in rather feebly. She had time to notice that Grandpa wasn't playing it their way. He looked solemn and was shaking his head slowly.

"You know—these youngsters nowadays—really!" he said finally, dividing his head-wagging between the Inspector and the Major. And a clever move, Peg thought.

Mrs. Bing-Birchall pulled down the front of her slouch hat, swung her cloak round angrily, and shouted, "I can see nothing—nothing whatever—to giggle at. Really—what next? Inspector Crope?"

"Leave this to me, madam. Now then—what's your first name, young lady?"

"Peg."

"Well, I'll give you a word of advice, Miss Peg. When a police officer asks you to explain something, never laugh like that. Half the suspects I've ever known laughed just like that—just the same phony sound—"

"But I'm not a suspect," said Peg.

"Then don't behave like one."

James evidently thought he should come to her rescue, even if it was risky. "Peg was laughing because what Mrs. Bing-Birchall saw was our old dog—"

"That's right," Robin cried eagerly. "Just our old dog, y'know, sir."

Major Rodpath had sat down close to where James was standing. His shotgun rested against his knee, and he had just lit a cheroot. But this talk of a dog shocked him into action. "What—that poor devil of a dog again!" He glared round. "You're not fit to own a dog. First, you put a rug over him, nearly suffocating the wretched animal. Told you then you ought to be ashamed of yourselves. Next thing we know—" Here he hesitated and had to appeal to Mrs. Bing-Birchall. "What were they doing?"

"Marching up and down this room. But it wasn't a dog. As I said, it was a creature—and a most *extraordinary* creature—"

"Don't let's get off the point," the Major told her severely.

Mrs. Bing-Bang was nearly purple with exasperation. "I'm *on* the point, so don't be so absurd. I say—a most *extraordinary* creature—"

The Major waved this away. "Their old dog, you see —poor old fella? And this is what I'm talking about. Downright maltreatment of a dog. Always makes my blood boil. Always—blood boiling. And I must say, I'm surprised at you, Professor."

"You needn't be," said Grandpa coolly. "I don't like dogs."

Major Rodpath could never have heard this before. It staggered him. *"You don't like dogs?"*

"No. Too fussy. Demand too much attention. It's always like having a drunken man in the room."

"Good God! I never heard such dam' drivel. Why—a man can't have a better, a more faithful, a truer companion than a decently bred dog. A man has only to understand a dog—"

But Mrs. Bing-Birchall had had enough. More exasperated than ever, she shouted, "Major Rodpath, will you please—*please*—stop talking about dogs?"

He stared at her in amazement. "But that's what we *are* talking about, isn't it?"

"No, it is not. Inspector Crope, you really must assert yourself."

"Just what I was about to do, madam. Now then—Major Rodpath, sir—just one question for you. Did you actually see this dog?"

"No. He was under the rug when I was here before. Thought I'd explained that. I told them then it was no place for a dog. You can't expect any dog—"

"No-no-no," Mrs. Bing-Bang shouted, looking half out of her mind. "Not back to dogs again!"

Inspector Crope held up a hand—a very large hand, too. "But, in fact, sir, you didn't actually see the dog—"

"I don't have to see a dog to know that it's being badly treated. Come, come, Inspector!"

"But you're missing the point, sir. Perhaps there wasn't a dog."

"Of course there wasn't." Mrs. Bing-Bang was shaking with fury. "How many times do I have to tell you? They were marching up and down with an extraordinary creature."

Robin's turn this time. "That was our old dog—dressed up."

"Dressed up?" The Major was shocked again. "A decent, faithful old dog! What you three need isn't dressing up but a good dressing down."

"Perhaps you're right, Major," said Grandpa very smoothly. "But you must make some allowance for teen-age high spirits. Don't you agree, Inspector?"

Behind a long, hard stare, the Inspector spoke slowly and suspiciously. "Up to a point, I do, sir. But is it a case of teen-age high spirits? Was it just a dog dressed up? And if it was, then where is this dog? Why not let us have a look at him?"

He was looking at Peg now, so she had to gabble a reply. "I'm sorry but you can't. The poor old thing was so cross about being dressed up and being made to march on his hind legs that he broke away and ran straight out."

"Not through these closed windows, I hope. And still dressed up? And still looking like the extraordinary creature that Mrs. Bing-Birchall says she saw?"

Feeling he was about to be too clever for her in a minute, Peg muttered, "Well—yes—I suppose so—"

Inspector Crope smiled for the very first time. It was the smile of a man looking at a small pork pie he was about to eat. And when he spoke, it was with a kind of grim relish. "Then if your dog isn't dead by this time—shot—he soon will be. Your poor old dog—dressed up to look like a monster—and dead as a doornail!"

Peg did her best. "Oh—that's terrible!"

"Terrible!" James was a mere echo.

Robin tried harder. "I think that's rotten luck."

Inspector Crope was now a man looking at three small pork pies he was about to eat, and he was enjoying himself so much that Peg could have slapped his great lump of a face. "Now I'll tell you what I think. Young people who've had a dog for years don't take his death as easily as you're doing. They don't just pretend to feel something. *Terrible—rotten luck*—t-t-t-t-t! You've given yourselves away."

"Very neat, Crope!" Major Rodpath barked. "Dashed clever, in fact!"

As the Inspector gave Peg, James, and Robin a look and a nod each, he also contrived, without appearing to be making a move, to put himself nearer the cupboard. Peg daren't exchange glances with the boys. "So I think that if you have a dog, then he's still here," he told them. "And if you haven't a dog—and can't produce one—then it must be something else—"

"Of course!" Mrs. Bing-Birchall shouted at him. "Most extraordinary creature! Told you twenty times!"

The horrible Crope was now actually close to the cupboard. It was like a sinister conjuring trick. He said very softly, "Just a moment, please, madam. I think I hear something moving in this cupboard."

He bent down and put his ear to it. Peg and the boys had time now to exchange glances of alarm. Peg looked at Grandpa, too, but he was calmly smoking his pipe and even appeared to be rather sleepy.

"Oh—yes, there's something moving inside this cupboard." He was no longer bending down. "So now I'll take a look."

"There is such a thing as a *search warrant*," said

Grandpa, very quietly, "isn't there, Inspector? I seem to have read about them."

"Quite right, Professor. There's also such a thing as a general district emergency, which provides me with a general warrant. I might also remind you that Major Rodpath is a Justice of the Peace." He tried the cupboard doors. "Locked, eh?" He looked around. "All right, I'll trouble one of you for the key."

The boys, saying "Key?—Key?," tried to put on a bewilderment act. Peg thought she could do better and said, "Oh—that cupboard hasn't been opened for *ages.*"

"It hasn't—eh?"

"No, I can hardly remember—"

He stopped her. "You aren't a bad liar, Miss Peg. But you're not a very good one either. Some stuff's been taken out of this cupboard during the last hour or so. How do I know? I'll show you." He bent down and began pointing. "I'm not Sherlock Holmes—but I know those spangles and bits of colored paper and straw can't have been there very long. In fact, hardly an hour, I'd say."

"First-class, Crope!" cried Major Rodpath. "Devilish neat!"

"Now if you won't hand over the key, I can if necessary force the doors." And then in a terrifying flash he sounded very angry. "Now let's stop this nonsense. Give me the key."

Robin ought to have felt as frightened as Peg did, but somehow he managed to assume a nonchalant air, as if he were bored and about sixty. "Oh—well, Inspector Crope, if you're ready to smash our cupboard doors just to look at a lot of old raincoats—you might as well have the key." And he handed it over very slowly, like a man delivering up his purse to a highway robber. Peg decided she ought to be braver—and cheekier.

Mrs. Bing-Birchall was furious. "If there's nothing in there but old raincoats, why did you have to tell so many stupid lies?"

"We just enjoy being deceitful," said Peg.

"Perfectly true, I'm afraid," said Grandpa, shaking his head. "Lying for lying's sake."

"Then you ought to be ashamed of them, Professor Hooper."

"I am."

Major Rodpath glared at him. "No wonder the country's going to the dogs."

"Why, Major," said Grandpa, "I thought you liked dogs."

"With respect," Crope began sternly, "I'd be much obliged if you'd all keep quiet for a minute or two."

As he carefully opened the cupboard, Mrs. Bing-Birchall and the Major went nearer, while behind their backs Peg, the boys, and Grandpa exchanged signals of alarm and despair. Then Peg jumped up to peep, so did Robin, but James and Grandpa never moved. The cupboard doors were open now. No Snoggle, though, just the screen of coats.

"What did I tell you?" cried Robin, cheekier than ever. "Just a lot of old macs and raincoats."

The Inspector, enjoying himself again, turned on him. "Then what's worrying you, boy?"

"I'm not worried," Robin declared bravely but squeakily.

"Yes, you are. Hear it in your voice. I'm good on voices. Have to be. And this is a deepish cupboard. Moreover, I heard something moving—and it wasn't raincoats. So let's see."

He was about to part the coats and look behind them —and Peg felt herself drowning in despair—when an inspired James staged his wonderful rescue act, afterward famous in the annals and legends of the Hooper family.

"Look, look! There it goes!" he was shouting excitedly, rushing toward the windows carrying a shotgun. He fired twice, making a tremendous and terrifying din, then shouted again. "Saw it distinctly—round sort of creature —metal scales—can't mistake it!"

He had turned them all away from the cupboard of course, and there was a lot of excited shouting.

"That's the creature," from Mrs. Bing-Birchall. "After it—hurry—hurry!"

"Which way was it going?" the Inspector shouted.

"Over to our left," James told him.

"Give me that gun, boy." And Major Rodpath snatched it from him. "Straight into action, Crope!"

"Yes, sir," said the Inspector, already on the move. He called back over his shoulder, "And you four stay here."

"Not me," said Robin as the three hunters hurried outside. "I'll follow 'em—and then report."

Chapter 8

First Interplanetary Dance

Peg, feeling a tremendous sense of relief, flopped onto the sofa, while James, the hero, sprawled in the old basket armchair. It was wonderful not having those three monsters and their guns cluttering up the place. And with Snoggle still safe, too.

"James," she said, "you were *absolutely fab*. Wasn't he, Grandpa?"

"He was indeed."

"Felt I had to do something," said James, who, as Peg knew only too well, was often very vain and boastful but now took the gentlemanly English stiff-upper-lip and no-fuss-please line.

"You know, James," Grandpa observed thoughtfully, "if you'd merely shouted, I don't think it would have worked. It was firing that gun that did it. That was an inspiration, my boy."

"Thanks, Grandpa. Major Rodpath had left it just beside me; otherwise I could never have rushed toward the windows with it. And of course in another few seconds old Crope would have found Snoggle."

Grandpa laughed. "And would then have told him that anything he said might be taken down and used in evidence against him."

"Or pulled the trigger of that ferocious rifle he's carrying," James added.

"No!" Peg protested. "Let's talk about something else."

"OK, sister!" James was no longer the modest English hero and had reverted to his American gangster style. "But just kinda remember, kid, all I've done is to buy ya a little more time."

"Ya can say that again, Mac." This was from Grandpa, who'd never talked in this style before. As they stared at him, he continued, "Don't look so surprised. I read some of this stuff in bed occasionally. But now I think we'd better make good use of the little more time James has offered us. I doubt if he'll be able to rescue us again at the last moment. We're still facing those two problems—how to keep Snoggle away from Crope and Co.—and how to get him back to his spaceship. Any ideas, James?"

"Not a clue about getting him back to the spaceship. That's baffling. Unless of course Robin and I put him in the wheelbarrow, cover him with old sacks, then wheel him in the direction of the spaceship and dump him as near as we can get to it. No?" This was because the other two were shaking their heads at him.

"Bound to be spotted almost at once," said Grandpa. "You'd never get through."

"Hopeless, James," Peg told him. "All we can do is to keep hiding him until we have a good idea about the spaceship. Perhaps they'll send for him," she added, though she couldn't make it sound really hopeful.

James pulled a face. "Those advanced spaceship types probably write off Snoggles. As Robin said—probably they can make dozens of 'em any time they want to—"

"No-no-no! I won't listen to that miserable stuff—"

"All right, Peg, all right! Let's leave that and concentrate on hiding him from Crope, who'll be back—I'll bet you anything. Well of course the cupboard's *out—*"

"The cupboard is *not* out," Peg declared firmly.

"Are you dotty?"

"Anything but."

"But Crope made straight for the cupboard—"

"And what gave us away," said Peg, "was shutting and locking the doors. I was dead against it—you remember, Grandpa? As soon as he saw we didn't want to open the cupboard—and we began telling him all those rubbishy lies—he knew we'd put Snoggle in there. If we'd done what I wanted to do, if we'd left the doors wide open, Crope would never have given it a second look."

"I'm bound to say, James," Grandpa told him, "I agree with Peg there. He'd have seen a lot of raincoats, thought the cupboard was used for nothing else, and then have gone to search the house."

"Of course," said Peg. "And when he comes back—and I'll bet anything he *will* come back—the only safe place for Snoggle is exactly where he is now, behind the coats with the cupboard doors wide open. He'll look everywhere except in that cupboard again."

"Sounds quite mad to me," James grumbled.

"I like it," said Grandpa. He tried to smoke and chuckle at the same time and ended with a little coughing fit. But he held up a hand to show that he'd more to say. "It's an impudent bold bluff, and I'd enjoy bluffing Inspector Crope, who's far too pleased with himself. Peg get's my vote."

James looked annoyed for a moment but then grinned at them both. "OK, we'll risk it. At least we can sit around here, with one eye on Snoggle, while the great

Inspector has to search the house from top to bottom. Hello, Robin's coming back. Now what's the news?"

Robin had obviously been running and came in quite breathless. "Going to get a drink of soda or something. Doubt if they'll be back for—at least—quarter of an hour or so. They've separated—across the fields—and are still searching. Must drink something—mouth's dry as an old bone—" And off he went into the kitchen.

Just as if he knew he was safe for some time, Peg thought, Snoggle came through his screen of coats and stood just inside the cupboard, his enormous eyes moving and flashing.

Even James was impressed. "When you haven't seen him for some time, old Snoggle really is *something.*"

"Of course he is—aren't you, Snoggle?" cried Peg. "And I believe he knows when it's safe for him to come out. He's really very clever in his own peculiar way."

"He wasn't very clever when he made a noise and Crope was listening," James objected.

"I've been thinking about that." This was Robin, back with his drink. "And I've a science-fiction sort of theory. Suppose Snoggle didn't care about making a noise and being heard just because he knew you'd rescue him, James?"

"Now wait a minute—"

But Robin wouldn't. "It's just a theory. But what if Snoggle, perhaps through one of those things on the top of his head, knows what's going to happen a few minutes before it does happen? I mean, he'd be able to know a bit of the future—"

"Then it wouldn't be the future, you chump," said James.

"You see what I mean, Grandpa?"

"I think so, Robin. His present time—his *now*—would be much wider than ours. But you and I will talk about that later, my boy, when this spaceship crisis is over and done with—"

"Yes, let's. But another thing, Grandpa. What if I— Robin Hooper—brought a spaceship here because I wished so hard—?"

"Never mind that. It's silly anyhow," said Peg impatiently. "Look at Snoggle. He's come out and he wants to play—to try another march—or something. After all, it's terribly boring for him in that cupboard."

They all looked at Snoggle. And nobody could deny that he was not only out of the cupboard but also moving his big fat feet or paws up and down. His eyes were very bright, too, as if he was ready for some caper.

"Ol' Snoggle sure is rarin' to go," said James, now a sheriff in a Western. Then, abandoning the character, he went on, "But don't forget, Peg, the stuffiness inside that cupboard suits him. We'll have to close the windows if he stays out, even if it's only for a few minutes."

"Not only that," said Grandpa, "but it's too risky having Snoggle out here, with all of us staring at him, if nobody's keeping watch outside. If you boys want to stay, then I'll go and be the lookout."

"Sorry—but that's a bad idea, Grandpa," Robin told him. "You'd look all wrong, and you wouldn't be able to see as far or move as fast as James and I can. No, James, I'll go. I rather like it out there, and while I'm keeping a lookout, I have some very interesting thoughts. But make sure the windows are shut, James. And if I see them coming back, Grandpa, I'll warn you at once, so you'll have lots of time to hide Snoggle."

Peg was concentrating on him now. He was looking at her quite expectantly, she thought, as he moved his feet or paws up and down, like "marking time" in drill. She felt there couldn't be any doubt at all that he wanted to play some simple little game.

She said this to Grandpa, while James was still making sure the windows were tight shut. "The point *is*, Grandpa," she went on, "that when he was marching with us before, he was happy just because he was doing something with us—wasn't any longer only a strange weird creature in a different world—"

Grandpa nodded and smiled. "*Communication*—a term very much in fashion now. You and Snoggle have discovered you can *communicate*, which is something an ex-student of mine told me, the other week, that he and I couldn't do. Probably Snoggle's no more addicted to marching up and down a room than you are—he may have the most fantastic hobbies and pursuits—"

"But I thought the idea was"—and this was James breaking in—"that he was some sort of pet—"

"I still believe he is, but in a society very different from ours. A kind of dog there, but to us a super-dog. Now let me make my point," Grandpa continued, "because both Peg and Snoggle are beginning to look impatient. It's not that they want babyish little games—what's important is the fact of *communication*—"

"Of course it is," cried Peg. "And we want to start communicating again—so just keep quiet, you two, and watch."

Peg marched a few steps, in the same deliberate style as before, and Snoggle kept step with her as he'd done before. When they had done this four times, it was Snoggle and not Peg who astonishingly brought in a variation.

When they turned, instead of marching back with her he stayed where he was, simply marking time. Then when she turned again and moved toward him, he sidestepped several paces and marched down alone. Then when he turned and she came toward him, he sidestepped again.

She gave a little scream of joyful excitement. "Look-look-look! He's doing a kind of Snoggle dance."

Moving only a few paces forward and backward, both of them did side steps now, more or less doing a kind of simplified tiny square dance. Grandpa and James began clapping for them.

Grandpa didn't often shout, but now he did. "It's the first interplanetary dance in world history."

"In the history of the solar system, I'll bet," cried James, clapping harder. But then he stopped. "Look, Peg, I'm sorry," he called. "But I think you have to turn it up now."

"Oh—no! I'm going to invent another little dance."

"Not with Snoggle. Look at him, Peg. He's nearly all in."

"It's true, my dear," said Grandpa. "He's beginning to look exhausted."

And he was, as Peg discovered to her shame. "Oh—Snoggle darling, I'm sorry—all my fault! He's closed his eyes, too. Does it mean he'll have to go back into the cupboard?"

"Best place for him now," said James.

Grandpa agreed. "And we couldn't have kept him out very much longer anyhow, not if Inspector Crope's going to pay us another visit."

"I was getting ready to push him in," said James, near the cupboard, "but now look—he's turned round—yes,

and he's walking in—no more being pushed backward for old Snoggle!"

"But he won't be able to turn round inside, behind the coats." Peg went closer to watch him. What he did was to turn round when he reached the coats, which didn't worry him because they were light and hanging loose and he was so solid and heavy. Now the front half of him bulged between coats, and he kept opening and closing his eyes. He looked rather miserable, and all of a sudden she felt even more "miz" than he looked. Just as if she were now a million miles away from the surprise and fun of their little dance.

Most people have their own way of dealing with themselves when they are feeling thoroughly depressed, and Peg's way was to award herself a piece—but not a large piece—of nut milk chocolate. She kept a secret store of it up in her bedroom, well out of the way of the boys, who could gobble their way through a whole bar of it in ten minutes. She went up, took one of the three remaining pieces, and started nibbling at it in a slow, sad kind of way as she returned downstairs. Not wanting to talk or to listen to the other two talking, she walked straight across to the playroom windows and stared out.

"Anything wrong, my dear?" she heard Grandpa ask.

"Feeling miz," she replied, without turning round.

Though kind and very sweet, Grandpa wasn't very good about moods, perhaps because he was so old. So now he persisted when even the boys would have kept quiet. "Miserable, eh? Because you had to stop your Snoggle dance?"

"Not just that." She still kept staring out of the window, not looking at anything in particular but champing away at the last bits of nuts. "It's everything. Weighing me down like a ton of black muck and rubbish."

"You ought to write a poem about it, my dear."

If it had been anybody else but Grandpa, she would have told him to shut up. As it was, she muttered, "Sometime perhaps," not caring if he couldn't hear her. And then as she went on staring, without noticing anything out there, there came through the dreary blankness of her low spirits a feeling that was very much sharper and really frightening, as if she were being warned that something awful might soon be happening.

And not more than a minute later, she saw Robin tearing toward the house as fast as he could. She began unfastening a window for him. "Robin's coming back," she called to Grandpa and James. "Full speed. Bringing bad news."

Chapter 9

The Other One

Peg let Robin in and then carefully fastened the window after him. He was out of breath, sweating hard, but instead of being red-faced, he looked quite pale. Peg wondered if he'd suddenly been taken ill. "What is it, Robin? You're not feeling sick, are you?"

"In a way—yes," he gasped. "But that's not—why—came back—"

"Well, take it easy, boy," said James, putting a hand on his shoulder. "You're not going to tell us that Crope and Co. are coming back at a gallop."

Robin shrugged the hand away to go and collapse on the sofa. "No—lost sight of them. Something else—quite different. You know—that short, deep ditch—just beyond our railings—but this side of the tennis court?"

"Yes—what about it?"

"Where I lost a shoe once—you mean?" said Peg.

Robin nodded, looked from one to the other of them, ran his tongue round his lips, then said, *"There's another Snoggle in that ditch."*

"Oh—jumping Moses!" cried James.

Peg made some sort of noise that didn't make a word.

"Are you sure?" asked Grandpa. "No, that's a silly question. Of course you are."

"Yes—and I wish I wasn't," said Robin earnestly. "It's not at the bottom of the ditch. If it had been, I don't think I'd have seen it. But there's a sort of ledge or shelf halfway down, and it's there, where there's just room for it. I think it must have rolled down after it was hit and somehow clutched some of that brambly stuff to stop itself."

"It's been *hit?*" Grandpa said that, but Peg and James said something like it.

"Yes." Robin at this moment seemed much older than his thirteen years. Somehow after that first wild entry he had forced himself to be quiet and serious and a reliable reporter of facts. "I think it must have been hit by some wild potshot from a rifle. Nobody was stalking it, or else it would have been found. But it's hurt—wounded I suppose I ought to say—but how badly I wouldn't know. There's some thick dark-green stuff oozing out of it—"

"Oh—no!" cried Peg.

"Nasty," said James. "Is it just like our Snoggle?"

"It's a bit smaller. Not quite so round and eggy. And instead of four antennae—or whatever they are—on top, it has three—and in a different arrangement. And now I'll say one thing—and this'll appeal to you, Peg—and that is, I don't believe now these Snoggles can be machines. They're creatures—like us, even if they do look so queer. When I was looking closely at this one—which I didn't enjoy doing, but I felt I had to—it opened its big eyes, very slowly, and gave me a sort of appealing look, just as if it knew I was feeling friendly and desperately sorry for it. Well, that's about all I can tell you." He looked at Grandpa. "So what do we do about it?"

"We bring it here," Grandpa replied at once.

"Grandpa," cried Peg, "I love you."

"Even if we can't doctor the poor creature," he continued, "at least we can give it the air treatment—cutting down the oxygen—that our Snoggle needed. What do you say, James?"

"I'm with you two hundred percent, Grandpa."

"I hoped you'd say that," Robin told them. "But I must warn you—it's not going to be easy. First, we have to lift him out of that ditch—"

"Oh—come on!" cried Peg impatiently. "We can't waste time talking—"

"Hold it, Peg! I don't think you ought to be in on this —the first sight of him nearly turned me up—"

"Oh—pooh and fiddle-faddle to that! If you could stand it, Robin, then I can. I'm coming with you, and that's that."

"But if Grandpa's coming, too—"

"And I certainly am, my boy—"

"Then there'll be nobody left here—"

"All right then, there won't," said Peg, more impatient than ever. "We'll have to risk that, and we shan't be so long away. But let's go and not sit around here just talking."

"Now wait a minute, Peg, and come off the boil," James told her severely. "We could waste more time dashing off without a plan than if we talked a bit longer here. I've been thinking. If we took that big rug—the one we've used for our Snoggle—and wrapped it round your chap, I take it the four of us between us could hoist him out of that ditch—right, Robin?"

"Yes. We'll just have to be careful, that's all. It's badly hurt, don't forget. Then we've also got to hoist it over the railings—and that'll be worse than the ditch. It may be a bit smaller than our Snoggle, but even so I'll bet it's heavy—"

"You needn't. I'm taking that into consideration." James was now in his solemn-planning mood. "Hoisting the creature over the railings is *out*. But then we don't need to. You're forgetting our gate into the field. And what we do is to take the wheelbarrow. We wheel *it* or *him*—"

"Let's say *him* now," Peg suggested.

"OK! We wheel him, still wrapped in the rug, through the gateway and then straight here. What happens after that, we don't have to decide now. Any comments?"

"Super idea, James!" And Peg, burning to be useful at once, went on, "One of you take the rug. I'll run round to the back and get the wheelbarrow. I'll go this way so that I don't have to unlock the back door. And hurry, hurry!"

The wheelbarrow lived in a small shed, full of gardening stuff, just beyond the back door. It was maddening in there, not only because it was rather dark and terribly cluttered with garden things, but also because like most people in a frantic rush Peg made everything more difficult for herself. Making a dash at the wheelbarrow, which had things in it and larger things leaning against it, she smashed a flowerpot, got in a tangle with trowel, fork, shears, and a leaking bag of smelly muck, and finally brought down a rake that hit her foot as if it wanted to take some toes off. Oh—if she'd only played it cool, as James would have done!

She limped out with the wheelbarrow, determined now to be calm and careful. It was easy enough crossing the lawn, but after she'd opened the gate into the field, it wasn't easy at all. To begin with, it was one of those very lumpy fields that must have been neglected too long. Then the wheelbarrow, which she hadn't handled often before, began to be awkward, wanting to go somewhere she didn't want to go, suddenly stopping altogether and then trying to rush away in a wrong direction. But even so, she did a lot of thinking, most of it grotty. First, however, she felt that this new wounded one ought to have a name, if only because this would make it easier to think about him, and finally decided, after trying out several names, to call him *Snagger*. So what then if Snagger died on them? Did they give him to Crope? And if not, after hiding the body in the cellar, would they have to wait until late—and she could see it happening at midnight— and then dig a grave and bury him—just like being in a horror film? And even if Snagger lived—and she very much hoped he would—then how about getting him back to the spaceship? But then, how could they get Snoggle back to the spaceship?

When she finally arrived at the ditch, Grandpa and the two boys were already there. "Thought you were the one who was in such a hurry, young Peg," said James, not playing it very cool now, in fact looking rather hot and flustered.

"I half killed myself in that garden shed, getting the wheelbarrow out. How's Snagger? That's his name now— Snagger. Have to call him something."

"OK—Snagger then," said James. "And he isn't a pretty sight, poor old Snagger. But you won't see the worst of it, because when Robin and I got the rug under him, we turned him round. Now then, Grandpa, I vote we stick to my original plan." James was obviously in one of his masterminding moods. "Robin and I go down again, ready to push him up. But before we start pushing, we hand you and Peg two corners of the rug each, and when we push, you pull. But you may have to bend over a bit, so be careful, Grandpa. Then as soon as what's it— Snagger—is safely on top, we all give a lift together and heave him into the wheelbarrow. All right? Come on, Robin."

Snagger might have been smaller than Snoggle, as Robin said, but all the same he was an awful weight. James's plan worked, but there was one dreadful moment when Peg thought she was going to slip, let go of her corners of the blanket, and ruin it all. But she didn't. Poor James and Robin lifted so hard that they looked as if they might burst. Then at last Snagger was safely on top. He had rolled a bit in the blanket, and Peg caught a horrible glimpse of his closed eyes and that dark-green blood-stuff that Robin had described.

All four were out of breath. And Grandpa, not smoking for once, was coughing rather alarmingly. "We'll rest a minute," said James, very much the man-in-charge. "Then one good heave and we'll have him in the wheelbarrow. And then—as that man at the farm always says— *Bob's your uncle!*"

"One good thing," said Robin, after wiping his face on his shirt sleeve, "there's no sign of Crope and his lot. We'd see them from here."

"Yes, but I've been thinking," said Grandpa, his coughing fit over. "What if they crossed to the road, had a car there, and decided to drive up to our front door?"

Peg took alarm at once. "And we don't know what to do with poor Snagger when we get him home."

"One thing at a time, if you don't mind," said James

sternly. "Now let's lift him into the wheelbarrow. We take a fat corner of the rug each, both hands—then heave when I give the word. Ready? *He-ea-ve!*"

That worked, too, to Peg's immense relief because she had wondered if the rug would stand the strain. But now Snagger was in the wheelbarrow—at least the main part of him was—and she and Grandpa tucked the rug all round him while the boys got ready to wheel him away, taking a handle each. It wasn't easy even for them over the bumpy field, and, walking alongside, Grandpa and Peg had to keep pressing down, to make sure poor Snagger wasn't jerked out of the barrow. Once they reached the gate, which Peg stayed behind to close, the boys could move easily ahead.

"But what happens now, Grandpa?" Peg asked as they crossed the lawn together, behind the boys. "I don't mean taking Snagger into our room. They can wheel him in. But what do we do with him then?"

"I've been giving that some thought. It's really the Snoggle problem all over again. We might settle it in exactly the same way. If there's enough room at the back of that cupboard for two of them, then that's where he must go. And thank the Lord these creatures aren't like Mrs. Bing-Birchall—and can enjoy stuffiness!"

The boys hadn't taken the wheelbarrow into the room. They had stopped just outside the windows, and Peg ran to join them, wondering what they seemed to be staring at. It was Snoggle. Not only had he moved out of the cupboard, he was standing in the middle of the room, looking toward the windows.

"He *knows*, you see," said Peg. "He's been expecting us to bring Snagger. That's why he came out of the cupboard."

"Unless he was just bored," said James.

"Well, something's exciting him now. Look!" And Robin pointed. "Two of his little masts—antennae—are lighting up."

"Yes, they are," cried Peg. "That must mean something very special, don't you think, Grandpa?"

"Certainly, my dear. No doubt about that. But as to what it means, what it's doing, we haven't a clue."

"What it isn't going to do," said James, in charge once more, "is to help us to get this other one—Snagger—out of this wheelbarrow and into a good hiding place."

"You don't know," Peg told him excitedly. "It might."

"Come and heave—and stop talking rot. Now then!"

Peg had time to notice that Snoggle had backed to give them room and that two of his little fat masts were still lit up, perhaps even a bit brighter. James now decided to keep Snagger wrapped in the rug, like a big parcel, and said that each of them must put one hand below and one above, a hand to lift and a hand to keep him steady. "OK! One-two-three-lift!" and in two ticks they had Snagger in his rug safely on the floor.

"Y'know, James, he wasn't heavy at all this time," said Robin.

"Of course he wasn't," cried Peg triumphantly. "And it was Snoggle. *He* did it somehow. He can make himself heavier and lighter—remember what he was like on the stairs—and now he's just done it for Snagger. And you can't deny it."

"No, I agree," said Grandpa. "There really is something in this, James."

"I don't say there isn't, Grandpa. But it's a waste of time talking about it now. We have to put poor old Snagger somewhere—quick as we can, too. Peg, you brought the wheelbarrow, so you'd better take it back to the shed."

She did a lot of wondering as she wheeled it round the back of the house. Would Grandpa convince the boys that the cupboard was the best place for Snagger? And if he did, would there be room in the cupboard for two of them? Not feeling ready for a hot argument or indeed for a disappointment about the cupboard—she still couldn't help remembering that horrible glimpse of poor Snagger —she cheated a bit, not perhaps quite deliberately loitering but doing what angry workmen described as "working to rule." So once in the shed, she carefully put back everything that had been in the wheelbarrow before and everything that had been leaning against it. Then she walked instead of running back.

Snoggle and Snagger couldn't be seen. James and Robin were half inside the cupboard, with Grandpa looking on. He turned to give her a cheerful nod. "It looks as if they just fit in, Peg. I wish we could do something for that poor creature instead of just jamming him into the back of a cupboard. But we can't risk keeping him out if there's any possibility of Crope coming back. Well, boys?"

They were out of the cupboard now, having carefully adjusted the screen of macs and raincoats. "OK at the back," said James. "Just enough room for them. And if Snoggle knows any more magic, he'd better start working it for poor old Snagger. Here, Robin, you fold up the rug —hiding those nasty green patches—and put it in a corner somewhere. We're leaving these cupboard doors wide open, Grandpa, trying the big bluff. I'm still not entirely sold on this whole idea, but we can't waste time arguing. It's a bind not knowing where Crope is and what he's up to."

"I'm thirsty," said Robin. "Want some soda, James?"

"Yes, but I'll get it myself." Exit boys noisily.

"Don't you want something to drink, too, Peg?" asked Grandpa, who was now filling his pipe.

"No, not now—later. But what about you?"

"It's about this time that I usually take a little whisky," said Grandpa, rather wistfully. "But I'll postpone it for half an hour, by which time I'll believe that Inspector Crope has decided to leave us alone."

"He hasn't, y'know, Grandpa."

"What do you mean, my dear?"

"I've just heard the front doorbell."

Chapter 10

Inspector Crope Again

The boys, still drinking their sodas, came back before Grandpa. "It's them all right," Robin announced gloomily. "Grandpa's doing his delaying bit so we can be all set."

"Yes—and listen," said James. "Peg, whatever you do, don't keep looking at this cupboard. Fatal! Keep looking up or down—as if Snoggle might be in the attic or the cellar. And, Robin, don't be cheeky."

"That lot make me feel cheeky."

"Well, keep it to yourself this time. Now—let's settle down and take it easy. They're coming."

All three arrived with Grandpa. Like an invading army again, appearing to fill the room with large strange bodies and guns. Peg tried hard to look as if she didn't hate them. James, she noticed, was looking loftily indifferent above his glass of soda, and Robin had put on his very innocent face—a bad sign because it meant he would soon be cheeky.

Mrs. Bing-Birchall, the pest, began sniffing and shouting at once. "Really! Look at those windows! Tight shut again! For goodness' sake, let's have some fresh air." And the next minute she had both French windows wide open.

Inspector Crope nodded his approval and then said, very softly, with a nasty smile all round, "But I can't believe this family really dislikes fresh air. Notice how warm they're looking, Mrs. Bing-Birchall. Curious, isn't it, they should keep such big windows shut tight? Unless of course they were afraid some creature might go scuttling out." He gave Grandpa a sly look. "Y'know, Professor, some of us aren't so green as we're cabbage-looking."

"Inspector," Grandpa began, smiling and looking interested, as if they might soon be talking about the elder Pitt and the Duke of Newcastle, "it must be years and years since I last heard that. And I don't suppose these youngsters even know what it means."

"I don't," said James. And sounded as if he didn't care either.

"Quite so." And Crope kept on with his cat-talking-to-mouse voice. "But you know how two and two can make four, I imagine. Now let me put a few points to you. Now it's quite true that one of the farm men down there"—and he pointed over to his left—"thought he winged one of the creatures, but then it disappeared. But our young friend here—James, isn't it?—couldn't have seen that one. And he couldn't have seen one just outside here—otherwise we'd have seen it when we ran out. He fired at nothing. Yet he described the creature, just what Mrs. Bing-Birchall thought she saw. And he could describe it because he'd seen it, here in this room." He gave each of them a look now. "You and your old dog!"

"All lying like the devil!" barked Major Rodpath bitterly.

"And I must say," Mrs. Bing-Birchall shouted, "I'm surprised at *you*, Professor Hooper."

"So am I, madam, but I'll continue, if you don't mind. You see, Professor, I knew you'd all been telling me a pack of lies ten minutes after I left here. I didn't come straight back because I'd some reports to collect and phone to county headquarters."

Peg didn't believe this, and when she glanced at Robin, she saw that he certainly didn't believe a word of it.

"Now, Professor, I'm no Red Indian or Zulu, but I can follow plain tracks when I see them. This creature left its tracks right up to these French windows, and there wasn't a single mark on the grass to show it ever left again. But of course that was half an hour ago. So now I'll take another look. No, Mrs. Bing-Birchall, Major Rodpath, you'll oblige me by staying here and keeping your eyes and ears open." And the Inspector marched out.

"Please, sir," Robin said in his mock-innocent voice, "could I watch the Inspector examining the tracks?"

"No, boy. You stay there." Major Rodpath could do a squinting glare, and now he did it. "Don't trust you fellas an inch. All that dam' nonsense about a dog!"

"To say nothing of not wanting to breathe any decent fresh air," Mrs. Bing-Birchall shouted. She looked hard at Peg, who longed to make a face at her, and then even harder at Grandpa. "I really am surprised at you, Professor Hooper."

"Yes," said Grandpa mildly, "you mentioned that before. But then, even at my age, I'm occasionally surprised at myself. Aren't you?"

"Certainly not."

"Neither am I," said Major Rodpath. "Always been a fella who knew his own mind."

"Have you, sir?" Robin, pretending to be about eight, piped up. "I haven't."

"Different thing altogether—boy your age—entirely different." The Major turned to the windows. "Well, Inspector Crope, anything new out there?"

"No tracks of a creature moving out, but two tracks of a wheelbarrow—quite new."

"A wheelbarrow—eh?" Cunning barking now from Major Rodpath. And he even half closed his eyes to be cunninger. "Some jiggery-pokery there, d'you think?"

"Possibly, possibly not, sir." He did another Crope look-round. "But the footmarks by the deeper track of the wheelbarrow suggests something was brought in and not taken out. May be another attempt at bluffing—"

"But of course, Inspector"—and it was James this time, not Robin—"mightn't we have taken something out in the wheelbarrow and left the wrong footmarks by walking backward?"

"If you'll keep quiet and listen, young man, you'll soon learn how much notice I'm taking of that silly question." Crope waited a moment, then became brisk and businesslike. "Now, Mrs. Bing-Birchall, I'll be very much obliged if you'll cover the front of the house. Keep a sharp lookout, please. You don't have to have your finger on the trigger, but I wouldn't have it too far away."

"Inspector, it will be a pleasure." And Mrs. Bing-Birchall left them.

"Now, Major Rodpath, if you don't mind, I'd like you to keep watch on this side, placing yourself where you can cover both that back door and these French windows."

"Get the place sewn up, eh? Sound work, Inspector!" And off he went by way of the French windows.

Crope sent a triumphant grin on a little tour round the four of them. "That ought to show you there's going to be no hanky-panky."

"Please, sir," Robin piped up, still aged about eight, "what's *hanky-panky?*"

"It's what you've been up to your neck in, lad. And don't give me any impudence. You're in no position now to be cheeky. I want all of you to understand there's to be no more fooling around. We mean business."

Peg couldn't resist it. "But I don't understand, Inspector Crope. When did the war break out?"

"That'll do, Peg," said Grandpa.

"But it won't do, Professor," Crope told him sharply. "They think they're playing games, and they're not, and I can hold you responsible. You've let these youngsters bring a dangerous creature in here—and—"

"Just a moment, please, Inspector." Grandpa took out his pipe and pointed with it. "How do you know this creature's dangerous?"

Crope was quietly patient, like the teacher of a dim-witted class. "Well, to start with, I'm a police officer, and I've been given my orders. Then again, these creatures have come in a spaceship from God knows where, some planet that probably wants to invade us—so of course they're dangerous—"

"I don't think that follows, Inspector."

"Why doesn't it?"

Grandpa now took over the class of dim-wits. "A civilization that can land a spaceship here, make it invisible, defend it by the use of some mysterious force—well, it must be a civilization far older and far more advanced than ours, with a technology far beyond anything we can understand—"

"I'll grant you that, sir, but are you trying to tell me this means it can't be dangerous?"

"I'm suggesting that, certainly—"

"And I'm not taking it," Crope replied firmly. "No, sir. We know a lot of things our great-grandfathers never knew. We're well in advance of them, you can say. But are we less dangerous than they were? Are we more peaceable and friendly to one another?"

"You're arguing that as we know more, then the worse we behave—um?"

"That's how it looks to me, Professor."

"All right. But when you apply your argument to these spaceship beings, there's a flaw in it. If their science and technology are so much in advance of ours, then if they were anything like as aggressive, greedy, destructive, and irresponsible as we are, they'd have ruined their world, probably finished it off, long ago."

"I take your point, Professor." Crope thought for a moment, then went on, dropping his voice a little, "But how do we know they haven't destroyed their world? How do we know that this little lot aren't roaming round, looking for another planet to settle on? And how do we know they couldn't wipe us out in half a day?"

"We don't know, Inspector—I agree. But the only evidence we have doesn't suggest they're hostile. And *we are*. As soon as the spaceship lands, we are. At least you and your friends are. You're quite ready to shoot and kill a harmless creature—"

"Stop there, Professor! Given yourself away, haven't you? Because what makes *you* think it's harmless? Now listen, all of you. I can see you think you've hidden this creature where I'll never find it. But I've done plenty of searching in my time—and if it's some size, if Mrs. Bing-Birchall's right—I'll find it. And don't try rushing it out from downstairs while I'm upstairs, because Mrs. Bing-Birchall and Major Rodpath are covering the house, and they're both good shots."

After giving them another severe look-round, he went on, "Now I could have two or three of my men here in ten minutes. To watch you closely. And I don't think you'd like having them here, would you?"

"No, we wouldn't," said James bluntly.

"Well then, all of you just stay right here—and don't get up to any more mischief. Professor Hooper, I want you to give me your word you won't let any of these three go roaming round the house while I'm searching it."

Grandpa gave him a gloomy nod. "I promise we'll all stay here until you get back."

"Good enough! Then you'll be out of harm's way." Crope took up his rifle, began moving, but then stopped to indicate the open cupboard. "I know one thing. I haven't to bother with that cupboard any more."

He went out without closing the door behind him. After a moment or two, James crept up to the door, made sure that Crope was making for the stairs, and then very quietly closed the door. "And now—what?" he asked, coming back.

Peg felt wretched. "Oh—it's hopeless. I could cry."

"No, turn it up, Peg," said Robin earnestly. "If you start weeping, we can't think—and we have to think, haven't we, Grandpa?"

"Well, I can think, too," cried Peg. "I've had some of the best thoughts there've been today."

"So you have, my dear," Grandpa told her. "Now

we've all got to think—and think very hard. And we've very little time left." He looked up. "No-no, Snoggle—get back! Push him back, James."

"You see," said Peg. "He *feels* the Inspector isn't here and that it's all friendly now—poor Snoggle!"

"Now, my dear, I'm going to sound rather callous and cold-blooded in a moment, but there's no help for it." Grandpa waited until she gave him an understanding nod. "We agreed earlier that creatures like Snoggle—and Snagger of course—aren't responsible for this spaceship. They're far more likely to be what we'd call *pets*. There could be various reasons why they were allowed to leave it. Being pets, they were let out to give them a change—"

"That's what I believe," Peg put in hastily.

"But they might have been sent out to test the atmosphere and conditions here, their spaceship masters considering them expendable if necessary. Or they may have been let out just to get rid of them—"

"Oh—no!" Peg again.

"All right. I don't like that any more than you do, Peg. And indeed we can't try anything at all unless we assume that Snoggle and Snagger are more or less pets and that those responsible for the spaceship want them back."

"Bang-on, Grandpa," said James.

"But I say"—and this was Robin, rather squeaky in his excitement—"couldn't they both—or at least Snoggle—be sending and receiving messages from the spaceship? Those four little mast-things on Snoggle's head must be used for something. Snagger's only got three, you remember, and he must be a bit inferior to Snoggle."

"We haven't to bother about that, Robin," said Grandpa. "No time now. I think it's safer if we assume that Snoggle needs some help, even if he is in communication with the spaceship. And indeed he may be completely out of touch with it. This means that somehow we must get a message through to the spaceship."

"But how, Grandpa—how?" Peg was showing signs of distress. "What can we do? *What can we do?*"

Crope's long wooden face came round the door, which he must have opened very quietly. "I don't know what *you* can do, but I know what *I* can do. And don't look at me like that, young lady—I'm only doing my duty. I tried upstairs first, just to make sure, but I was ready to bet money you'd take the creature down to the cellars, and that's where I'm going now. Stay here, all of you. Remember your promise, Professor—to keep 'em here."

"Don't worry about that, Inspector. They want to stay here. We're having a very important discussion."

"Then I'll leave you to it. Though don't imagine you can talk yourselves out of the hole you're in." Crope's face vanished, but he didn't close the door, and James once again made sure it was properly shut.

"I have an idea," said Grandpa very quietly. "I don't say it'll work, but it's our only chance. Come closer and keep your voices down."

Peg jumped up at once and then knelt by Grandpa's chair; the boys did the same; and now they were in a real conspiratorial huddle. "I like this," said Robin.

"Shut up—and listen to Grandpa," said James.

"We can't get near the spaceship. We know that," Grandpa began, in an exciting sort of whisper. "But we have to send a message—a very urgent message—telling them somehow that Snoggle and Snagger are here and are in danger. And if they knew that, we hope they'd find some way of rescuing these two creatures they brought here."

"I bet they would, too," cried Robin. "They're very, very clever."

"And I expect they *adore* Snoggle," said Peg warmly. "I do."

"We're getting off the point." James frowned at Peg and Robin, then looked at Grandpa. "How are we going to tell them?"

"The only way we can do it," Grandpa began slowly, "is by *thought pictures*. We know that one thing Snoggle shares with us is sight. We communicated with him through sight."

"And feeling," Peg said very quickly.

"Possibly, my dear. Anyhow, we concentrate. We remember. First, Snoggle—then Snagger. We hold in our minds the clearest possible pictures of Snoggle and ourselves. We *make the spaceship people see* Snoggle here. James, you saw Snoggle first—start remembering it as clearly as you can—"

"Righto!" And James bowed his head and put a hand over his eyes.

"Now me, please!" cried Peg eagerly. "I'll think and think about Snoggle marching, and then our marvelous little dance. I'll *see* it all—and then keep on and on— um?"

"Yes, Peg, on and on. Now, Robin?"

"Poor old Snagger for me, if you don't mind, Grandpa." Robin squeezed his eyes tight shut. "Finding him in that ditch, then helping to bring him here. And if they can't get my thought pictures, they're no good, those spaceship people."

"Let's all concentrate and remember, then."

It might have been two minutes later, or five or ten,

when Peg was startled by hearing the mocking voice of Inspector Crope. "Well-well-well!"

"Oh—rats to you!" Peg was furious. "Now you've ruined it."

"Big clot!" Robin was muttering. They were all looking at Crope now.

He was amused. "Ruined what? Were you holding a little prayer meeting?" He moved in a pace or two, still holding his rifle of course.

"No, no, Inspector," said Grandpa, quite smoothly. "Just trying a little experiment in interplanetary communication."

Inspector Crope was no longer amused. He looked and then sounded quite grim. "Well, let me say something before you go on with your experiment. It was an artful bit of bluffing, Professor, but I've just rumbled it. You've still got the creature in this cupboard, haven't you?" Then Peg saw his eyes widen in amazement. "No, you haven't. It's *coming out.*"

Peg jumped up and saw that not only was Snoggle out but also that coming out behind him, a bit shaky but with his eyes well open, was poor Snagger.

"Now you've torn it, idiots!" Robin told them bitterly.

"God in heaven!" Crope exclaimed. "*Two of 'em!* And just look at 'em! Eggs with eyes! And things on top lighting up! Unbelievable! But they're not getting out of here." And he hurried round them, to stand in front of the windows. He tucked his rifle into his right shoulder and began slowly to raise the barrel with his left hand.

"Oh—no!" And Peg burst into tears.

Chapter 11

After the Rescue

As Peg hastily dried her eyes and blew her nose, she realized that a number of different things, quite unexpected, were happening all at once. On the other hand, what she had expected—shooting from that terrible rifle of Crope's—had not happened yet. She noticed first that Snoggle and Snagger, with Snoggle a little in front, had moved two or three feet nearer the windows. Then, to her surprise, she saw that Inspector Crope, though he was still pointing his rifle at them, had backed and backed until he was now just outside the windows. At the same time she could hear a queer, creepy sound, rather like that electronic music they use in films to suggest other planets, and she could see a ray of light, greenish on the whole and trembling as it brightened, coming in through the windows. The sound got louder and went higher and higher, hurting her ears. The ray of light found Snoggle and Snagger, just as if it had been looking for them.

"Spaceship! Spaceship!" Robin was shouting.

Then something came, as fast and terrifying as a thunderbolt. There was a lot of argument among the Hoopers afterward about this rescue thing—what it was, what it looked like, exactly what it did. Peg always admitted she felt confused by the screaming sound, all the flashing light, her own tearfulness, but insisted that the creature —not a machine, as Robin and James always said it was —seemed to her like a huge but well-disposed metallic octopus, which was able to push into the room two or three arms or tentacles and a mouth arrangement that suddenly opened wide to admit Snoggle and Snagger. Then it withdrew, quick as a flash, and streaked off. Though afterward she called it *The Gobbler,* she knew it hadn't eaten Snoggle and Snagger but was carrying them safely back to the spaceship. One last thing—there had been a rifle shot as *The Gobbler* came in, because it had knocked down Inspector Crope, who had blindly pulled the trigger, firing into the air, before he passed out.

They went out to see if he was badly hurt, all of them sure that Snoggle and Snagger had gone back to the spaceship. "We did it, didn't we, Grandpa?" Robin squeaked jubilantly. "Our thought pictures, I'll bet anything."

"They may have helped, my boy," said Grandpa, "though we'll never know."

"Unless they send *us* some thought pictures. There's an idea. Why shouldn't they? After all, we looked after Snoggle and Snagger for them. We deserve *something.*"

"Never mind about that," said Peg. "The point is, Snoggle's not been left behind. He's safe now."

"Unless something happens to the whole spaceship," said James, who often liked to look on the dark side when Peg and Robin were being wildly optimistic. "Look, Grandpa—I don't think Crope's really hurt. Just had a shock, that's all. Doesn't know what hit him. I vote we take his rifle away until he knows what he's doing."

"Now then—now then—what—what!" This was Major Rodpath, who'd come trotting round the corner.

"You youngsters keep quiet," Grandpa muttered. "I'll deal with him—and Crope."

"Heard a shot, didn't I?" Major Rodpath was with them now. "Hello—what's happened to Crope?"

"We were just wondering," replied Grandpa, smoothly and easily. "Some sort of minor seizure, I'd say. We'd better take him indoors, Major. He can rest on the sofa until he feels all right again."

"Quite! Give you a hand. Jump to it, you boys!"

Once they had Inspector Crope lying on the sofa, he put a hand to his head, opened his eyes, closed them, and opened them again.

"How are you feeling now?" asked Grandpa, all concern.

"Blacked-out, didn't you, Crope old man?" said Major Rodpath.

The Inspector closed his eyes, then murmured something that nobody could understand. Grandpa took Major Rodpath to one side. "Do you think a little whisky might help?"

"Not straight after blackout, Professor. Might help us, though—ha—ha!"

James was sent to the dining room for whisky, soda, glasses. Everybody else stared at Inspector Crope, whose eyes were now wide open. After a few moments they focused on Major Rodpath. The Inspector was making a great effort. "Major Rodpath," he began slowly, "you saw them—did you?"

"Saw *what* old man?"

"Those things—creatures, sir—very peculiar—" Crope closed his eyes and put a hand up to his head again.

"What's he talking about?" the Major asked Grandpa.

"I can't imagine. Soda with your whisky, Major?"

"A touch, thanks. Afraid Crope's wandering. Seen it happen before. High blood pressure, ten to one. Cheers!"

Grandpa said "Cheers!" too, and they both drank their whisky and soda at the same time, looking, Peg thought, as men always did at these moments—solemn and idiotic.

"Professor Hooper—" And this was Crope, who was almost sitting up and seemed to have nearly recovered. "Professor Hooper—going to prefer charge against you—"

"Better take it easy, old man," the Major told him.

"Very serious charge. Much obliged you'd note this. Creatures. . . . Hindering police officer execution of duty . . ."

He closed his eyes. Major Rodpath looked from him to Grandpa, who shook his head. The Major nodded slowly. But then Crope, staring rather wildly now, started again.

"Very serious charge. Much obliged you'd note this, Major Rodpath, sir."

"If you feel up to it, Inspector—"

"They must have been in the cupboard—"

"Don't quite follow. What must?"

"Creatures I mentioned." Crope seemed to stare hard at the space just outside the cupboard where Snoggle and Snagger had been standing. But his manner was rather dreamy. "Like big tin eggs with crocodile feet. Lit up at the top—"

"I'm not following this," Major Rodpath whispered. "Are you, Professor?"

"Some confusion, I fancy—poor fellow! Big tin eggs coming out of the cupboard! Pity!" Some head-shaking again. Robin, in danger of exploding, stuffed a very

grubby handkerchief in his mouth and ran out of the room.

"Not really crocodile legs and feet—paws. But gives you some idea. . . . Certainly lighting up at the top . . ."

"Getting a bit much, isn't it?" the Major whispered. "Better offer to run him home soon—um?"

"Both of 'em," Crope muttered, "had *enormous* eyes—" His own, not enormous, looked for and found Major Rodpath. "Much obliged you'd note this, sir—"

"Not missing anything, Crope. Enormous eyes. Some of our fellas used to see 'em in Burma. Don't give 'em a thought, old man. Now if you feel up to it, I'm running you home."

"On duty—emergency duty," Crope objected.

"Not now—no. Not after nasty little blackout. I'll take responsibility. Professor, if you and the boys will get him up and bring him along, I'll take his rifle with my gun."

Peg followed the procession along the hall, but when she heard a shouting voice coming from the playroom, she hurried back and there ran into Mrs. Bing-Birchall. This was awkward, might even be dangerous, because this woman had seen Snoggle and so could tell Major Rodpath that Crope wasn't talking nonsense. So she must keep her here, and she did it, as she told the others afterward, really very cleverly.

"Oh—Mrs. Bing-Birchall—what's been happening? Do please tell me." Doing the eager, humble little girl bit.

"Devil of a lot, if you ask me! That wretched spaceship's in for trouble now, no doubt about that," Mrs. Bing-Birchall shouted happily. "Tried sending a rocket—just caught sight of it, quarter of an hour ago—but didn't do it any good. Our troops are moving in. Tanks, armored cars, the lot! Stood on a wall, used my field glasses, saw some of 'em myself. Heard a few planes high up, so no doubt the R.A.F. is joining in. Young fellow with a transistor set told me the Government's given spaceship an ultimatum—if they haven't gone by six-thirty, we blow 'em off the face of the earth. And serve 'em dam' well right, I say!"

"But how can we send a message to the spaceship?" said Peg. "How could we make them understand? They must be utterly strange creatures."

"Monsters of course. But we've some clever fellows in the Ministry of Defense. Have a cousin there, though he's a fool." Mrs. Bing-Birchall paused a moment. "Oh—yes, of course, Inspector Crope—Major Rodpath—where are they?"

"I'll explain in a minute, Mrs. Bing-Birchall. But wouldn't you like some whisky first? Grandpa and Major Rodpath have had some. Oh—good! I'll find a glass for you."

But when she went back with the glass, Grandpa, looking very solemn, had taken charge of Mrs. Bing-Birchall. "So Major Rodpath insisted upon taking poor Crope home in his—Rodpath's—car. Thought it better that a police driver shouldn't take him. But you hadn't been forgotten, Mrs. Bing-Birchall, and the police car's waiting to take you home. Ah—I see Peg's brought you a glass. Won't you help yourself? You know how much soda you like with your whisky."

"Not much, Professor, after a day like this," she shouted cheerfully. As she helped herself—"Not surprised Crope had a sudden blackout. Overdoes it, I'd say. Carries himself too stiffly—always dangerous sign. You suggest I don't call—eh?"

Grandpa had turned himself into a sort of bogus doctor. "I do, Mrs. Bing-Birchall. I think it would be more tactful to leave him alone for the time being. And if, as you say, the military have moved in, we need no longer worry about the spaceship—or its creatures. Or," he added slyly, after noticing she had finished her drink in two great gulps, "youngsters amusing themselves dressing up their dog."

As soon as Grandpa had taken Mrs. Bing-Birchall along to the front door, the boys immediately appeared from nowhere. They were masters of this very useful trick, able to fade away, vanish, and then return at once when people they disliked had gone, a trick the envious Peg was never quite able to work. Now she excited them by talking about the troops and tanks and armored cars arriving—possibly the R.A.F., too—and the ultimatum with the half-past-six deadline.

James alone had a watch. "That gives them only just over ten minutes."

"It's all rot," Robin declared quite angrily. "To start with, how could our chaps have gotten through to the spaceship people? And even if they could, what's the use of talking to people from another planet about half-past six? And anyhow, I don't believe our bombs and shells and bullets will bother the spaceship. Its people are much too clever. And what a rotten, stinking idea it is, attacking them instead of trying to learn something!"

Grandpa was back. "I agree with Robin," he announced.

"Then you think Snoggle will be safe?" Peg couldn't help feeling anxious.

"Somehow I do, my dear."

"Well, that's something. But now he's gone—and I haven't a single thing to remind me that he was ever here."

"Hard luck, Peg!" said James. "But then you couldn't have asked him for a lock of hair." And he and Robin guffawed at this, as they always did at their own silly jokes. She could have slapped them.

"Not funny—so shut up! Grandpa—if we'd only a photo of Snoggle. Doesn't matter about poor Snagger. But Snoggle—it's such a shame."

"Not as bad as you think," said Grandpa coolly. "You remember, Peg, you went to the kitchen to get tea ready, and it was several minutes before I joined you. The boys had gone to do some final clearing away of cupboard stuff outside. Well, I remembered my Polaroid camera, and when I came down with it, Snoggle had come from behind the coats and was standing, in a good light, just in front of the cupboard. And before I pushed him back, I took two shots of him—"

"Oh, Grandpa—super—gorgeous? Where are they?"

"Here's one." He brought it out of his wallet. "And this is specially for you, Peg." He handed it over.

She held it up so that the boys could see it, too. All three stared at it intently. "Oh—look at him!" Peg cried, enraptured. "Isn't that marvelous? You must admit there's something very *lovable* about Snoggle. Couldn't I have it enlarged, Grandpa?"

Robin got in first. "Yes, you could. And I'm going to have an enlargement, too. Otherwise, nobody'll ever *believe* me."

"I don't care about that," said Peg. "I just want to remember Snoggle when he's back in the Milky Way somewhere."

But Robin was bursting with excitement. "With a photo we could go on *television*—"

"You could, but you're not going to, Robin," said

Grandpa very firmly. "And for two good reasons. First, there's still Inspector Crope, who'll realize he was made a fool of and could still bring his charges. Your father and mother don't want a son whose name goes straight from the *Radio Times* and the newspapers to the office of the Director of Public Prosecutions—"

"Aw—Grandpa—couldn't we square old Crope—?"

"The second reason's even more important." Grandpa sounded severe for once. "I don't say you should never give an account of what happened today. But not yet, and not for some time. I'll tell you why, Robin. Certainly there'd be a tremendous fuss, not only here but perhaps all over the world. Probably you—or somebody representing you—would be paid a great deal of money. You'd be photographed, interviewed, made much of—"

"And I could have a big boat," Robin cried.

"What you'd soon have is a big head," James told him. "Sorry, Grandpa—go on."

"James is right. You'd soon be a small boy on an enormous mushroom. You'd feel unsettled for years and years and might never get over it. Your father would never forgive me if I gave you the slightest encouragement. Robin Hooper, my boy, there isn't going to be any publicity, any television, any agents and managers and fairy gold. And unless you give me a solemn promise, I'll have to ask Peg to hand back that photograph—"

"Oh no—*please*, Grandpa!" Peg almost shrieked. "I won't show it even to my very best friends—"

"Whoever they are," said James, who was always teasing her about changing her best friends.

But Grandpa, over the top of his spectacles, was still staring sternly at Robin, who had at first pulled a long face but was now looking solemnly anxious. "Have I your promise, Robin? This is serious, my boy."

"Yes, you have—honestly, Grandpa."

"Then Peg can keep the photograph."

"But when she takes it to be enlarged," said Robin earnestly, "what are those people going to say?"

"Not a thing," James told him. "They don't know what they're enlarging—and don't care—"

"I'll tell them it's just a joke," said Peg.

But what they heard then suggested that all jokes were over. The boys rushed outside. Even Grandpa hurried a little. Peg moved out slowly. She was too curious to stay indoors and not see anything, but at the same time she dreaded what she might have to watch. Once outside, she found it hard to tell what was happening. There was a lot of firing, some of it very loud indeed, and she heard James explaining to Grandpa and Robin that mortars and tank cannon were being used. She was furious. "Oh—the rotten, beastly pigs! The spaceship hasn't done *them* any harm."

"Quite so, Peg," said Grandpa. "But isn't it possible that nothing's really hitting the spaceship? Don't you think so, James?"

"I do," replied Robin promptly and proudly. "Spaceship people are too clever for 'em."

"Grandpa's asking me, not you." James waited a moment or two. "Of course we can't see anything properly, but it seems to me there's a darkish haze over there I never noticed before."

"Yes, there is," cried Peg. "And it won't be sunset for another hour yet. *Something's* happening over there."

"Well, perhaps by this time the pilots of the spaceship

know they've landed on a lunatic world," said Grandpa. "And they can protect themselves. And isn't it getting dark—or is it just my old eyes?"

"No, it isn't your eyes, Grandpa," James told him hastily. "There's a patch of darkness spreading and spreading—"

"And listen!" This was an excited squeak from Robin. "Firing's stopped. They've given it up as a bad job."

"Serve them right—horrible beasts!" Peg cried. "Spaceship—hurry up—and go now—go!"

"That's just what they're going to do." Robin was jigging with excitement. "Remember? When they came it was dark, and we thought it was because of the storm. Now I'll bet anything it wasn't. Somehow they made it dark."

"I believe you may be right, boy," said James slowly.

"And so do I," said Grandpa, excited himself for once.

"Look—look—look!" Peg screamed. *"They're going."* She heard again that strange, high whirring sound and saw once more that flicker of odd light. It was all over and done with in a few seconds, and then all four of them were staring silently at the evening light displacing that sudden artificial darkness. Grandpa gently squeezed her shoulder.

"Peg, my dear. Snoggle's gone home."

Chapter 12

Good-bye, Good-bye!

Peg felt that Grandpa's remark was really the end of the Snoggle adventure, not of course counting all the talk they would have about it afterward. Snoggle had gone home—and that was that. Now she had to think about supper, and as it was Robin's turn as well as hers, she marched him off to the kitchen. They also took turns in demanding the chief supper dish, and today being James's, he had gone all American and insisted upon corned-beef hash. Grandpa didn't think it suitable for an evening meal, and Peg was against it because it took longer than most of their supper things to prepare. But James, who could be very obstinate, would have nothing but corned-beef hash as his choice, and he'd been able to talk Robin over to his side. This was why Peg marched Robin off to the kitchen at once. If he was in favor of corned-beef hash, then he would have to start peeling potatoes.

"And we'll have to hurry up," she told him. "Otherwise, supper will be ages. Mashed potatoes are only the beginning of it."

"There's a machine now that peels potatoes," said Robin.

"Well, we haven't got one. And we'll need all these."
She dumped them into the bowl and then put it under
the tap. "This is the best thing for peeling. You start
while I make sure I can open this corned-beef tin, and
then I'll help you to peel." All of which was of course
very ordinary and boring after the spaceship-and-Snoggle
excitement. And Robin said as much just before Peg,
who'd done several little jobs, joined him at the potato
bowl.

"All the same, Peg," he went on as soon as she was by
his side, "those spaceship people have rather disappointed
me."

"Now why? You were the one who thought they were
altogether marvelous. *Gosh!—Gosh!—Gosh!* Remember?"

"OK, OK! I still think so. All the same, I can't help
feeling they might have done something about it."

"About *what?*" Peg was struggling with a particularly
horrible potato that was almost making faces at her. And
though she didn't mind Robin's going on about it all, she
wasn't anxious to say much herself.

"Thought pictures," he replied solemnly. "Look—why
were they able to rescue Snoggle and Snagger? Because
Grandpa having this super idea—we were able to tell
them, through thought pictures, where Snoggle and
Snagger were. You believe that, don't you, Peg?"

As a matter of fact she did. But she felt she ought to
be fair to the spaceship people and didn't want Robin to
turn against them. "We can't be sure about that, y'know,
Robin. For all we know, Snoggle and Snagger—Snoggle
especially—might have been sending messages to the
spaceship, using those antennae things that lit up. He
might not have needed our help at all. Though of course
I did say, almost all the time, that Snoggle somehow un-

derstood our feelings toward him. He *knew* we were friendly and other people weren't."

"All right, I agree with that. But I'm certain we *helped*—four of us together sending thought pictures. And either way I'm disappointed. If the spaceship people were too grand to send us a thought-picture message, just as a kind of *thank you*—OK—they couldn't bother about us, too busy getting the spaceship off. But in that case, couldn't Snoggle himself have done *something*—a sort of good-bye? But nothing, you see—not a sausage. That's why I said I was disappointed—"

"Just a minute, Robin." She tried to sound calm and cool, though her mind was racing. "We've done enough potatoes and I have the pan ready for them, and you know how long it takes to boil them properly. Here—pop them in!"

But even then she didn't want to tell Robin at once what she was thinking. "We'll lay the table first," she told him.

"How d'you mean *first?*"

"Before I explain. Come on. We can do it in two minutes." And she bustled about, doing far more of the work, not because Robin was lazy and unwilling, but because he was still brooding over the spaceship people.

When they had done all that could be done in the dining room and returned to the kitchen, she said, "We've plenty of time now, waiting for the potatoes, and I think the atmosphere will be right. So now—listen, Robin." She waited a moment. "Before, we were *sending* thought pictures—messages—to the spaceship—"

"Of course we were. I don't see—"

"Then just listen. You're disappointed because you haven't received any thought-picture messages from the spaceship. But that may not mean that nothing's been sent. We haven't been ready to receive anything—don't you see, Robin?"

"Peg, that's marvelous. I've been stupid and you're being clever. Of course—just as we had to concentrate on *sending*, now we ought to concentrate on *receiving*. Super, Peg! And this is just the right time to try. Only you and me here, and all quiet."

"Yes—and we sit well apart—don't speak at all—don't think hard about anything else—just remember Snoggle and Snagger and wonder vaguely about the spaceship. If we get nothing at all," Peg went on, "then we'll know they're not bothering about us—and that'll be that. But if we try, there's a chance we may get *something*. Now I'll sit here and you sit over there. And remember, Robin, you mustn't talk. Not a single word."

For the next ten minutes or so the only sound in the kitchen came from the water that was boiling the pota-toes. But then there was a huge explosive *Gosh!* from Robin.

"Oh—shut up!" Peg was really angry with him. "Now you've ruined everything. I won't see anything else. Nei-ther will you."

"I saw right inside the spaceship. Did you?"

"Yes, but I don't want to talk about it now."

"I do. I'm going to tell James and Grandpa—"

"No, you're not." She got to the door before he did, and she wouldn't let him push her out of the way. They were as close to a fight as they'd been for a long time.

"What's the matter with you, Peg? Have you gone dotty or something? I only want to tell James and Grandpa what I've seen—"

"I know—I know—and so do I. But not *now*—that's

the point. Robin—please—just listen a minute, that's all."
She had released him, and now he moved away from the
door, so that she felt that she could, too. "If we start telling them now, then supper will be late and probably
messed up, and everybody'll be cross and there'll be a lot
of arguing and contradicting and it'll all go wrong. You
can see that, can't you, Robin?"

"I suppose so—yes." He sounded rather grudging.
"But what I saw—what happened to me—gosh!—that's
fifty thousand times more important than dishing up
corned-beef hash on time—"

"It is to me, too, Robin. I understand exactly what
you feel. I'm just as excited as you are—inside. But if we
start running around trying to explain to Grandpa and
James *now*, we could easily mess it all up. But if we get
supper ready—and *then* tell them, we've a much better
chance of making them understand. You do see that,
don't you, Robin?"

He did, but he took his time about admitting it.
"Well, I suppose so," he said finally. Then he brightened
up. "But anyhow we can start telling each other, can't
we?"

Oh—dear! Now she had to tell him that wouldn't do.
She knew it would be far better if they saved everything
until supper had been served. After telling him this, she
cut the argument by doing a lot of bustling around, com-
bining impatience with importance, with the corned-beef
hash.

"Not quite brown enough," James told her, after taking a whacking great helping, "but pretty good all the
same, Peg. What's your verdict, Grandpa?"

"Rather unsuitable at this hour, though that's not
Peg's fault, as you insisted upon having it. But excellent

—quite excellent." He looked across at Robin. "Is this all Peg's? Or did you contribute, Robin?"

"Not very much, Grandpa. I was too excited." He gave Peg an appealing look. "Can I tell them now?"

Grandpa laughed. "I don't know what Peg thinks, but it's obvious you're bursting to tell us something—"

"Sticks out a mile, boy," said James rather patronizingly. "So you'd better get on with it."

Robin took a last forkful of the hash, hastily chewed and swallowed it, gave his plate a little push, and then announced dramatically, "I've seen inside the spaceship."

"I'll bet," said James scornfully. "Now I'll tell one."

"I did. Honestly, I did. And if you don't believe me, then ask Peg. It was her idea—the way we might do it—"

"Is this true, Peg?" Grandpa asked. He had been smiling, but now he looked serious.

So she explained about Robin's disappointment and how they had settled down and concentrated, this time to *receive* and not send thought-picture messages, and how it seemed to have worked for both of them. "I don't know what Robin got. I wouldn't let him tell me. I said we ought to wait until we could tell you and James as well. Also I wanted to make sure you wouldn't think we'd made it up together. I don't know what Robin saw, and he doesn't know what I saw."

"Well, I get the idea, Peg, and there may possibly be something in it," said James. "But as far as I'm concerned, it'll depend on what *you* saw. Robin's been so full of science fiction and spaceships for the last two years, I'd say he's only got to close his eyes and imagine spaceships by the dozen—"

"But he didn't imagine Snoggle, James," said

Grandpa. "Snoggle was solid and real enough. So you go ahead, Robin. You'll get a fair hearing from me."

"Thank you, Grandpa!" Robin waited for a moment. "I'll only give you an outline now. I want to sort out the details and try to remember them properly and then write them down. I started concentrating on Snagger because I'd found him and I could still see him clearly—poor old Snagger! Well, after a minute or two, I saw him all right—cleaned up and not looking badly hurt any more. And somehow he made me feel he was remembering me, really sending me a *thank you* message—"

"I'm sure he was, Robin," said Peg, daring to interrupt if only because Robin was hesitating a little.

"But it's not telling us very much," James protested, though not sneering at all.

"Give me a chance, fathead," Robin told him. "Snagger wanted to show me as much as he could. So he started moving around, so that I could see what he saw. There were three or four others just like him—that is, a bit smaller than Snoggle and with three antennae. They were standing in corridors or moving along them, though what they were doing, if anything, I couldn't discover. The corridors seemed to be made of some glassy stuff, and they were on different levels, with some kind of escalator arrangement in all of them. They weren't brightly lit, and I couldn't see any particular lights. It looked as if the glassy stuff provided all the light they needed. And now—to prove I'm not making this up—I couldn't see any machinery at all, and that's just what I'd expected to see —y'know, all sorts of strange elaborate gadgets, like our moon modules only more so. Mind you, I'm not pretending I was taken all over the spaceship, which was obviously enormous. I just saw what Snagger wanted me to see."

"And what did you hear?" asked James.

"I never heard anything of course because those creatures don't hear anything. They must use a mixture of sight and whatever those antennae things do. I saw some dials high on the walls and some different colored flashes that ran along the walls, as if they might be orders or messages. And I had a glimpse of a big central hall, and at one end of it, quite enormous, there was some sort of moving astronomical map, but of course I couldn't understand it. There didn't seem to be any windows in the part of the spaceship I saw. Mind you, it wasn't always very clear." And Robin looked round rather apologetically.

"I'll tell you one thing," said James. "I really don't believe now you made this up, Robin. If you had, it wouldn't have been so dull. There'd have been wizard machinery and creatures with three heads and eight arms. What d'you say, Grandpa?"

"Well, I haven't seen a lot of very advanced technology, James. But a few places I've visited where it's been at work always seemed to be rather dull and disappointing. Even so, Robin, don't tell us that the only creatures you saw were Snagger and his fellow Snaggers—come, come, my boy!"

"OK, Grandpa—I was saving them—the others I saw, just quick glimpses, that's all. And chiefly in that big central place, where one wall was a kind of map or chart. These other spaceship creatures or beings were of different sizes, some twice as tall as Snagger or Snoggle, a few three or four times as tall. Most seemed to have various arm arrangements, not eggy like our two. And the taller they were, the less solid they seemed to be, not at all the heavy lumps Snoggle and Snagger were. In fact, the very tallest seemed hardly there at all—you could almost see through them—"

"Yes-yes-yes!" cried Peg eagerly. "And they were the chief ones, weren't they?"

"I don't know. Were they?"

"Of course! D'you mind if I go on now, Robin? Sure?" Peg smiled and nodded her thanks. Then she looked at Grandpa. "I don't think I saw as much as Robin did. He's probably left out a lot of details, as he said he would. But if I didn't see as much, I believe I was much *closer* to it than he was. This was because I concentrated on Snoggle, who knew me better than poor Snagger did Robin. And you were quite right about him, Grandpa, when you said he must be in the spaceship as a kind of pet. Please, James, will you peel an apple for me, too?"

"I will. But aren't you going to be too excited to start eating an apple?"

"Yes, while I'm talking. But I'm not going to talk long. I want to think about it more, then perhaps do a long poem. Anyhow"—and Peg stopped to take a deep breath—"just as Robin began by seeing Snagger, I saw Snoggle —and as clear as anything. I really felt he was looking at me and that he knew, perhaps after he'd tried several times before, that at last I was looking at him. And don't raise your eyebrows like that, James. I can't prove I didn't make it up. All I can do is to tell you what I saw, what I honestly felt, and—this is the part you may not want to believe—what I felt really strongly that *they* were feeling."

Without thinking what she was doing, Peg took a bite out of the apple that James had peeled for her. So she stopped talking for some moments. It was deep dusk outside now, and the light above the dining table was on. Chewing her apple, Peg took in the scene before her as if every part of it were quite new and strange, so that a few days later she tried to write a poem about it.

"Who were *they*, Peg?" Grandpa looked all forehead under that light high above them. And his question wasn't a challenge but gently encouraging.

"I was coming to that, of course," she told him. "Snoggle soon began to let me see what he saw. As I said before, we were right in thinking he was some kind of pet, but now I knew he was also a very special pet. I knew that because he was in a very special place in the spaceship, not just in one of its corridors as Snagger seems to have been. I think this must have been the pilot's place—or where the important ones, in charge of the spaceship, could be found. It was a kind of curved-gallery place, with some sorts of windows high up and below them a lot of little colored lights winking on and off and changing. No, James, I know what you're going to say—just like the pilots' cabin in a jet plane, but it was far bigger and more elaborate. And nobody touched anything—"

"Had they anything like arms?" asked Robin. "Because as I told you, I saw some that had."

"There were three of these special people or beings or creatures or whatever you want to call them. Two of them had what you called arm *arrangements*, Robin, and the other one hadn't. They weren't like Snoggle of course, any more than a very tall, thin man is like a fat, little poodle. Yet they weren't utterly unlike Snoggle. They belonged to his world, just as the tall, thin man and the fat, little poodle would belong to our world. Do you understand?"

"Yes, my dear," said Grandpa. "I imagine you could

say they were very advanced developments of Snoggle creatures. Would that do?"

Peg gave him some pleased, rapid nods.

"Half a minute, though," said James. "I know about Snoggle of course, but how were these others, apart from being much taller, like him and yet not like him?"

"Well, they were like a Snoggle stretched to a great height—about ten feet, I'd say. And instead of being tinny, like Snoggle, they were kind of glassy, just as Robin said. But then, like Snoggle, they didn't have any separate heads and bodies. They had enormous eyes, even bigger than Snoggle's, and very beautiful, changing color all the time. And like Snoggle, they had those antennae things on top, but instead of having only four, as Snoggle had, they had—oh!—about a dozen, lighting up and changing color, as if they were all very busy about something. And now we come to the hard part—and if anybody laughs or says I'm making it up, I'll stop and never talk about it again—never! And I mean it." She looked round defiantly.

Robin answered first, squeaking with excitement. "Peg, I *know* it's true. I don't care what anybody else says."

"It all sounds a bit thick, sister," said James, though without mockery. "But please don't stop now, even if it gets thicker. After all, there *was* Snoggle—and there *was* a spaceship—even if you may be letting your poetic imagination run wild—"

"And we don't even know what imagination is," said Grandpa. "I knew a man—student of mine after the war —who thought he'd completely imagined a war story, and later it turned out that every incident in it actually happened. For my part, though, Peg, I'm ready to believe you saw what you say you saw—so go ahead."

"It isn't just seeing now," Peg began, very earnestly, "but what I felt—and felt so strongly that it's not possible for me to disbelieve it. One of those three superior beings —perhaps he was Snoggle's master—knew we'd tried to protect Snoggle, and wanted to show me he was grateful and friendly. So I was—you might call it—put through to him. I could see, quite closely, quite clearly, his enormous eyes, even bigger than Snoggle's—emerald green changing to dark green, light blue going down to indigo—oh marvelous! And for a minute or two—if you understand what I mean—he *thought* at me. It was just as if twenty different voices were telling you twenty different things all at the same time. I suppose I only got bits of what he was thinking at me."

It was obvious to the other three that Peg hadn't stopped because she needed their encouragement, that she was now trying to remember as much as she could, hurriedly putting the bits together. So they didn't speak but kept a steady gaze fixed on her, waiting for her to continue.

"What he made me understand was this. Their species had visited our earth a long time ago, and now they were taking another look at it, on their way to somewhere else. They didn't stay because they felt the hostility all round them. Just as if we'd landed a plane on a cannibal island. Snoggle and Snagger and a few other creatures hadn't been sent out to gather information—the spaceship itself had various better ways of doing that—they'd just been allowed out, for a change, just as we might let a dog out. Oh—and what I called *The Gobbler* wasn't a creature but simply a machine they'd assembled at once—and don't ask me how because I don't know—just to rescue Snoggle and Snagger."

"A kind of *instant rescuer*—um?" said Grandpa.

"Gosh!" cried Robin. "And I'll bet that was nothing to them. But, Peg, where had they come from—where was their planet? Weren't you told?"

"Oh—Robin—I wish this had been happening to you instead of me," Peg told him. "Though I don't think even you would have understood. All I could make out was it was somewhere in our part of the Milky Way—almost a sort of neighbor. But doing a special thought picture for me, he did let me have just a glimpse of it—"

"Gosh! Lucky you! What did their planet look like?"

"I only got a very quick glimpse. All I saw was a huge plain, darkish blue, with no big buildings, as if there were hardly any people or everybody lived underground. The sky seemed to be pinkish—and—" she added almost apologetically, "there seemed to be two different suns—one small but dazzlingly bright, and one on the other side, enormous but dark red and not bright at all. But it was all too quick, and I got the idea that his time and mine weren't the same, that they could slow up time or make it speed up just as they pleased. So he thought he was giving me a good long look at his planet when to me it was nothing but a hasty glimpse. And that's all I can tell you, though perhaps other things will come out in my poem." Trying hard to appear calm and cool, she went on, "Shall we clear the supper things now, Robin?"

"Oh—no, not yet. Hang on, Peg! Have a heart!"

"Well, I'm not going to have any argument about anything—not tonight." She didn't look at James, just at Robin.

"No, Peg. Something quite different. Just a question I want to put to Grandpa."

"All right, my boy, though I don't promise to be able to answer it. Some of your questions are a long way out of my depth. But go on—let's have it."

"Well, it's connected with this spaceship and what Peg and I saw. Now I'm fed up with science fiction stories all about solar systems—even whole galaxies—turned into empires, making war, invading each other, with fire and slaughter and death rays and all the rest of it—you know—"

"I can imagine," Grandpa told him. "Just projecting our hideous aggressive fantasies as far as the stars—"

"Absolutely," said James. "And as soon as a spaceship comes, we want to start banging away at it. OK, Robin—I can see you're bursting to ask your question—"

"Well then," Robin went on, "here's this spaceship from a distant planet. It belongs to a species far, far cleverer than we are, probably much older, too. OK! But they're not going to do us any harm. They're quite peaceful—"

"More than that," said Peg. "Really *friendly*, I'd say—"

"Granted, granted!" said James. "But come to the point—the question, Robin boy—"

"It's here, so don't interrupt, anybody. Mightn't it be more than just luck that the spaceship didn't come to do us any harm? Mightn't there be some sort of plan—perhaps a plan for the whole universe—that just wouldn't allow creatures from one part of the galaxy to visit other parts if they weren't peaceful and friendly, if all they wanted was invasion and conquest and mad empires? What do *you* think, Grandpa?"

"If there is such a plan, it isn't working very well on this planet—"

"No, Grandpa, but I meant as between planets—and solar systems—which might be such a long way apart on purpose—"

"I know, Robin." Grandpa hesitated a moment. "I've sometimes thought there might be a plan for everybody and everything in the universe. If there isn't, then the whole thing's idiotic—even more idiotic than we humans are, because at least we can sit here quietly and talk about a plan. But then our idea of a divine purpose behind the razzle-dazzle of atoms and molecules would itself be part of the universe, wouldn't it?"

"It would," said James. "But take it easy now, Grandpa. Let's just say there might be a plan for everybody and everything—for the four of us—"

"And Snoggle," Peg put in hastily.

"And poor old Snagger," Robin suggested.

Grandpa had been lighting his pipe. After a few preliminary puffs, he smiled at them. "*And*—don't forget—Mrs. Bing-Birchall, Major Rodpath, and Inspector Crope."